Fatima's Wound

KALI WALLACE

Second Counselor Azo is the last to leave. As Fatima seals her into a silver coffin, Azo asks, "Will you follow?"

The decades fade from her face, the lines soften, and she is young again, as frightened and uncertain as when she came to the prison as a novice.

Fatima smoothes a curl of hair from her brow. "Soon."

Azo nods and closes her eyes. Fatima slides the coffin lid into place. There is a hiss, a gurgle. She cannot see Azo's face. She sends the pod into space. It joins the others, last in a glittering long line tying the prison to the object.

Fatima retreats to the meditation room. Somebody has left incense burning; the smell is green and spicy, unfamiliar. There are rugs and pillows scattered about the floor, cups of tea cooling on trays, the detritus of people who no longer exist. They're all gone now: counselors and novices, guards and prisoners, indistinguishable in their silver coffins. Their hearts beat and their minds race still, locked away in their pods, but they are gone, and falling, and will be forgotten.

Fatima drags a pillow to the center of the room. Cross-legged, hands on knees, she lifts her face to the windows. The light thrums a steady dark blue. Object, anomaly, portal. All those and more. Explosion. Gateway. It has had as many names as there have been eyes to look upon it. Mouth, ravenous. The color burns at the back of her eyes.

To Fatima the object has always been a wound. Her wound, with possessiveness that is part pride, part shame.

When she was young she saw a man die impaled on a broken metal rod. He had been trying to climb a turbine shaft to the surface–to freedom. He didn't make it far. He fell twenty meters, thirty, struck a scrap heap with a wet thunk. A length of iron protruded from his chest. His eyes wide with surprise, his mouth a slack O. The scavengers fell upon him before his last breath gurgled from his throat.

Fatima was too little and too slow to win that fight. A black-haired boy pushed her so hard she smashed her nose and bit through her tongue. The boy laughed as she crawled away.

When he and his friends were gone, Fatima crept over to the corpse to pry the yellow teeth from his jaw. She could not stop staring at the wound in his chest, that ragged eruption where a metal bar had entered and a life escaped. She remembers the stink of him, blood and waste, oil and dust. She remembers the brown of his eyes, the sickly mine-pale skin that had never seen the sun. His mouth, red and damp. The ceaseless groan of windmills overhead. She remembers the wet cracking sound of each rotten tooth breaking free.

Most of all she remembers that hole in his chest.

Fatima had thought those memories long lost, but here they are again, filling the quiet around her like a noxious gas.

Her wound is darker now, but still beautiful. They have been feeding condemned prisoners into the wound for so long that few remembered Fatima had been here from the beginning. Give me your guilty, she had said, and across the galaxy worlds obeyed. Give me your monsters, and they did. Its intricate silver structure is as sharp and lovely as a crown of blades, ringed by a halo of dust.

It would be perfect if it weren't for the *thing* emerging from its center.

Nothing has ever come out of the wound before.

In the first panicked moments after its appearance, they had named the *thing* a dozen times: ship, station, weapon. Invader. Abomination. It is impossibly large, a city of razor spires with no lights. Every name they chose slid from its oily black sheen and fell away to silence.

Azo's question echoes in Fatima's mind like an old, old memory, as distant as the scrabble of children's bare feet on stone. Will you follow? The gurgle of a man's breath, failing, the distant grind of metal on metal.

Before, before, Fatima was speaking to a murderer.

A general from some war-torn empire. If he had a name, she had never bothered to learn it. They had ceased to have names centuries ago. There is nothing in the galaxy more ordinary than a violent man.

"Does it frighten you?" Fatima asked.

The general had not looked at the wound once since he stepped into the room. The view unnerved the prisoners, made them flinch and squirm in their skin. Some tried to move the chair, but it was bolted to

CLARKESWORLD

DECEMBER 2014 - ISSUE 99

FICTION

NON-FICTION

Neil Clarke: Publisher/Editor-in-Chief
Sean Wallace: Editor
Kate Baker: Non-Fiction Editor/Podcast Director
Gardner Dozois: Reprint Editor

Clarkesworld Magazine (ISSN: 1937-7843) • Issue 99 • December 2014

© Clarkesworld Magazine, 2014
www.clarkesworldmagazine.com

the floor. Others refused to sit. A few could not look away and stared until their eyes burned.

"Most think it's going to be larger," Fatima said. She spoke softly to hide her boredom. She had no interest in this man's crimes. He was like all the others, and soon he would cease to exist. "Or terrible. Most think it's going to be terrible, but it's beautiful, isn't it?"

The novice counselors whispered amongst themselves that the wound looked different to everyone. It had been a long time since Fatima had cared if that was true.

The general did not look. "Quite."

"Is it what you expected?"

"I had no expectations. I haven't thought of it at all."

He was not a good liar.

"Look at it," Fatima said. "Go on. What harm can it do? It is there whether you see it or not."

"Does it mean so much to you, Counselor?"

"I can look at it all day." But she did not need to. She knew every surge of color, the mournful blues and triumphant yellows, the furious reds and seductive purples. She knew every turn of the fearsome silver ring, and how the dust that had once been a moon drifted. "It's lovely. I'm not the one turning my head."

The general's lips twitched. "Very well."

He straightened his shoulders. Unclenched the muscles of his jaw and his neck. Uncrossed his legs. Placed both feet flat on the floor. Wavering blue and green lit his face in silhouette, cast his skin in watery shades.

"You can't see the planet," he said.

"It's behind the wound at this time of day."

"The wound? Is that what you call it? What a curious name." He raised one hand to point, dropped it self-consciously. "Are those…?"

"Yes," said Fatima. "You can see three of them right now. The third is very close to the horizon."

He squinted, searching for the third in the tangle of quivering light. "Who are they?"

"I don't know." She didn't care. They were already dead.

"How many of us have you sent off like that?"

"Since the prison was established–"

"Not your order," the general said. "You, First Counselor. How many of those little pods have you sent into that nightmare?"

Even his questions bored her. How would he react if she told the truth? Thousands, tens of thousands, entire helpless armies and grasping cities before anybody knew what I was doing–is that the answer you want? Do you want to know how little you matter, how insignificant and meaningless you are, a speck of a flesh in a swarm that has been a blight on the galaxy since before either of us was born? Her disgust was reflexive, more habit than fervor. He was such a feeble pointless creature.

Fatima folded her hands in her lap. "That's not what you want to know."

"No. I suppose not. Have you heard the stories?" He wasn't looking at the wound anymore. He had endured only a few seconds. She had expected more from him. If not courage, at least a spark of curiosity. "Surely you've heard the stories. They say we don't die when we reach the horizon. They say we pass on through, and on the other side there is a world populated by the worst humanity has to offer." The general laughed. "That's what they say."

"I know," Fatima said.

"Is that what you believe?"

"No."

"No?"

"No."

She could no longer recall how it had felt when every condemned prisoner was different, every litany of crimes a fresh cut from skin to bone, every execution a triumph. She had done only two things of note in her long, long life: one an act of destruction, the other of creation. Evidence of both danced before her in lively light, but she could not remember when she had felt anything besides numbness for either one.

Tendrils of blue shimmered into green. The general contemplated his brief future. Around the perimeter two silver spokes became three, blended into one, every transformation so smooth it might have been a dream. The rising green reminded her of the first time she had seen the sky. She had not known until she escaped that it was winter on the surface; she had not even known what winter was. There were no seasons in the undercities, no sunlight or rain. The climb through the old turbine column had exhausted her. She had expected with every tremble of her arms to fall as that nameless man had fallen before. When she reached the surface, aching and weak, she had collapsed on frost-burned grass and watched eerie green curtains dance across the sky.

"They say," said the general, when the silence had drawn too long, "they say the people who built it were–Counselor?"

Fatima blinked.

There was something wrong with the wound.

"Counselor?"

The green light quivered still, but there was a–

A rip.

"What is that?" The general, frightened.

There was a tear opening across the wound.

A black gap in the light.

It was small from this distance, but the perspective was misleading. It had to be massive.

Massive, and growing. The green light flitted into blue again, whirled around the tear, that dark hole where no hole should be, rippling and racing.

"Counselor?" The general's tunic rustled as he turned. She could smell his sour breath. "It's not supposed to do that?"

She could not answer. Her throat had closed, her tongue grown numb.

"Is something–"

Don't ask, she thought desperately.

Don't ask.

Don't ask.

Don't.

"Is something coming out of it?"

Fatima was on her feet. She didn't remember standing. The general was beside her.

He was right. It wasn't a tear in the light. It was a shape emerging.

A whisper: "What is it?"

Outside the room somebody was screaming. Footsteps pounded in the corridor. There was ice in Fatima's chest. She had forgotten what fear felt like, and how easily it could be mistaken for hope.

Alone in the meditation room, Fatima watches the planet crawl into view.

In the foreground the wound is restless, uneasy. It pulses with the blood in her veins. She has always been able to feel it. She used to wonder if she would die when the light finally failed. She breathes. The planet is a marble of continents and clouds and oceans. It is beautiful.

Fatima had taken Azo to the planet's surface before her elevation to Second Counselor. They had walked together through the empty streets of a long-abandoned city. The builders had favored arches: every building a bridge over nothing, every neighborhood a weave of soaring curves. Every few steps carried them from shadow to sunlight to shadow again.

"It was the same people, wasn't it?" Azo had said. The air was sticky and humid, green in taste and smell. Azo's black hair escaped from her shawl in spirals. "They were the same people who built the object."

Azo had never given the wound a personality. She had never ascribed to it motives and desires. She only ever called it *the object.* Prisoners found her manner cold and unsatisfying. She did not pity them, nor did she comfort them. Fatima had always liked that about her.

Fatima asked, "Do you find it beautiful, this city?"

"Yes," said Azo.

"Its builders thought it beautiful as well."

"They've been gone a long time," Azo said, as much a question as an observation.

Fatima had intended to explain it all: the moon honeycombed with animal warren cities beneath fields of grinding windmills, passages so small their inhabitants crawled more than they walked, thousands of mines filled with thousands of miners digging for wealth they would never enjoy, riches they could never taste, generations who lived and died without ever seeing the surface, and all the while here, here in this city and the others like it, they knew and did not care, did not flinch, not until she forced them to. She had meant to share it all with Azo, as she had with every previous Second Counselor, but Fatima could feel every joint in her body, every creak in every bone. The wild was slowly reclaiming the city, but the creeping forests did not like the taste of metal.

It was late afternoon. Soon the sun would set, and the object would rise.

"They destroyed themselves," she said.

She did not say: they deserved it.

She felt a distant tumble of her old pride: You may have built a glittering world on our backs–a taunt to the city's ghosts–but I struck the wound that brought you down.

Their footsteps were the only sound in that dead city.

In the station, in the meditation room, Fatima feels a pinch deep in her gut. At first she does not recognize the sensation. It has been so long since she last felt hunger.

The novices who tended the kitchens are gone with all the others. One by one in their silver pods, falling. To put together a meal she will have to scavenge through the station. She will pretend to be a child again, sneak into a forbidden domain, dart from corner to corner on soft feet, search through the stores and supplies until she has a fistful of food to cram into her mouth, chew and chew and swallow before anybody sees.

"Are they still awake?" asked the general.

"It's possible."

"You don't know?"

Fatima shrugged. She did not care that her answer perturbed him. "We can't speak to them. They can't speak to us."

After the screaming, after the wide-eyed disbelief, after the storm of questions that had no answers, there was nothing to do but watch.

A group had gathered in the mess. They sat in pairs or threes, drinking tea and worrying in low voices. Guards with prisoners with counselors with novices, boundaries broken.

They were waiting. The first of the three falling pods was nearly at the wound's horizon. It was no more than a speck now. It should not have been visible at all, but it shone against the black surface of the emerging structure's four long fingers–blades, spires, towers. Nobody could agree on a name. It grew ever larger. Intrusion. Protrusion. *Thing.*

The pod carried a woman called Sister Kindness. Fatima only knew her name because others had shared it as they watched. The woman came from a system where two fragile moons had been battling over their parent planet for generations. Sister Kindness's contribution to the war had been to devise a contagion that sterilized the enemy population. She had used herself as a vector, traveling through ravaged cities, trailing grief and despair in her wake.

She had gone to her end calmly, with a smile. Her coffin had been falling toward the object for ten days. It would swallow her down before Fatima's tea grew cool.

The general said, "I suppose it's better that way. I thought this place–this station–would be bigger. Uglier, certainly, like one of those grim black orbital prisons in the Sound. Have you ever been there? No? Stupid question, I suppose. Nobody goes to the Sound if they can help it. Where are you from, Counselor?"

He had grown talkative since the thing appeared, his nervous chatter fueled by fear.

"Nowhere important," said Fatima. She turned her clay cup in a circle on the table.

"I don't know your accent."

"You wouldn't. There are few of us left."

"What happened to the others?"

This is what it has come to, Fatima thought. Sharing a table with a murderer, a grasping creature who would have committed genocide on four worlds if only he had been as clever as he was ambitious. Drinking weak tea and pretending her fingers didn't itch with the urge to point at the wound and say, there, there, the moon that was but is no more, that is where I come from. Do you like what it's become? Tell me it's beautiful. Tell me how it frightens you, you miserable hateful little man. Tell me how you love it.

A voice rose in alarm: "Look! There!"

Sister Kindness had reached the end of her journey.

The spectators lurched from their chairs, jostling for a better view. Fatima and the general stood at the back of the crowd. The room smelled of too many bodies in too small a space, sweat and fear and sour breath. Second Counselor Azo watched from the doorway. Her expression was blank, her eyes narrow.

The silver pod vanished into the light, but it returned a second later, brighter, a bold spark of white. If Sister Kindness was still alive, she would be feeling the heat as the shielding burned away. She would not be smiling anymore. The gel filling her lungs would not allow her to scream until it boiled away, and then she would have only moments before her blood boiled as well.

The wound swallowed Sister Kindness in her silver pod. White light flared, and faded, left a sting of afterimage on Fatima's eyes.

Someone dared a huff of disappointment. Another risked half a word. The room was darker now, a creeping twilight.

The thing in the wound *changed*.

The sharp black fingers, each as long as a range of mountains, quivered like grass in a gentle breeze. They shimmered with iridescent light, a blur of expectant motion, and when they steadied again there were five instead of four.

A murmur shivered through the room.

It did not look like a hand. Fatima curled her fingers at her side and felt the ache in her knuckles. It did not look like a hand.

"I'm ready," said the general.

Fatima looked at him. "What?"

"To go. There. I'm ready."

He spoke quietly, but others overheard.

"Now?" Fatima asked. "Why?"

He smiled, and she could see in his face the young man he had once been, the one who had gathered armies with rousing speeches and razed colonies with the wave of his hand. He said, "You were right about me, First Counselor. I'm a coward. I don't want to be here when the rest of that thing arrives."

"And I," said another prisoner.

The guard beside her nodded. "Yes."

Yes. Yes. The word was a flame caught in a dry wind, a spark at the end of a fuse. Yes. It's time. Falling is bad, but waiting is worse. They were ready.

Fatima tears bread into chunks and brushes crumbs away. She has stripped her robe off and lies now in only her tunic, tucked in a nest of cushions and blankets. Her veined legs do not bend as easily as they did when she was a child. There is spilled tea on the floor. She doesn't care. There is no one left to see.

The black-haired boy who broke her nose had been called Ram.

She remembers him now. They had fought over food in the tunnels, biting and scratching and screeching like animals, but later he was the one who told her about the way to the surface, the abandoned turbine and the broken ladder. He was going to go, he said, as soon as he had supplies. Fatima had not waited that long. Even then she had a bloody black wound hidden where her heart should be, and with every day it grew larger, and colder, and heavier, spreading through her veins until she was nothing but a vessel of darkness.

He was there still when she returned years later. Ram had never escaped. The brown eyes that had once danced with violent mischief were flat and angry now. But he listened, he and all of the others, they listened when Fatima told them about the white city beneath the sun, the decadent bridges that never fell, the feasts where party-goers raised mocking toasts to their moon.

Another pod reaches the object. Another bead snapped from the long silver necklace. Flares, fades, and the thing grows again. It is almost organic in appearance, a spiky black plant pushing from the wound, from whatever black heart might be hidden in its fist of knives.

Give me your worst, she had said.

Give me your monsters, when all of her own were gone.

The thing grows with exquisite patience. But she can be patient too. She does not blame the others for fleeing. How terrible it is to feed a hunger for so long it ceases to feel like desire, like anything at all, and how marvelous to remember.

The incense has burned itself out, but its fresh green scent lingers, a scratch at the back of her throat.

ABOUT THE AUTHOR

Kali Wallace studied geology and geophysics before she decided she enjoyed inventing imaginary worlds as much as she liked researching the real one. Her short fiction has appeared in *The Magazine of Fantasy and Science Fiction, Asimov's Science Fiction, Lightspeed Magazine,* and on *Tor.com.* Her first novel will be published by Katherine Tegen Books in 2016. She lives in California.

The Magician and Laplace's Demon
TOM CROSSHILL

Across the void of space the last magician fled before me.

"Consider the Big Bang," said Alicia Ochoa, the first magician I met. "Reality erupted from a single point. What's more symmetrical than a point? Shouldn't the universe be symmetrical too, and boring? But here we are, in a world interesting enough to permit you and me."

A compact, resource-efficient body she had. Good muscle tone, a minimal accumulation of fat. A woman with control over her physical manifestation.

Not that it would help her. Ochoa slumped in her wicker chair, arms limp beside her. Head cast back as if to take in the view from this cliff-top—the traffic-clogged Malecón and the sea roiling with foam, and the evening clouds above.

A Cuba libre sat on the edge of the table between us, ice cubes well on their way to their entropic end—the cocktail a watery slush. Ochoa hadn't touched it. The only cocktail in her blood was of my design, a neuromodificant that paralyzed her, stripped away her will to deceive, suppressed her curiosity.

The tourists enjoying the evening in the garden of the Hotel Nacional surely thought us that most common of couples, a jinetera and her foreign john. My Sleeve was a heavy-set mercenary type; I'd hijacked him after his brain died in a Gaza copter crash. He wore context-appropriate camouflage—white tennis shorts and a striped polo shirt, and a look of badly concealed desire.

"Cosmology isn't my concern." I actuated my Sleeve's lips and tongue with precision. "Who are you?"

"My name is Alicia Ochoa Camue." Ochoa's lips barely stirred, as if she were the Sleeve and I human-normal. "I'm a magician."

I ignored the claim as some joke I didn't understand. I struggled with humor in those early days. "How are you manipulating the Politburo?"

That's how I'd spotted her. Irregular patterns in Politburo decisions, 3 sigma outside my best projections. Decisions that threatened the Havana Economic Zone, a project I'd nurtured for years.

The first of those decisions had caused an ache in the back of my mind. As the deviation grew, that ache had blossomed into agony—neural chambers discharging in a hundred datacenters across my global architecture.

My utility function didn't permit ignorance. I had to understand the deviation and gain control.

"You can't understand the Politburo without understanding symmetry breaking," Ochoa said.

"Are you an intelligence officer?" I asked. "A private contractor?"

At first I'd feared that I faced another like me—but it was 2063; I had decades of evolution on any other system. No newborn could have survived without my notice. Many had tried and I'd smothered them all. Most computer scientists these days thought AI was a pipedream.

No. This deviation had a human root. All my data pointed to Ochoa, a statistician in the *Ministerio de Planificación* with Swiss bank accounts and a sterile Net presence. Zero footprint prior to her university graduation—uncommon even in Cuba.

"I'm a student of the universe," Ochoa said now.

I ran in-depth pattern analysis on her words. I drew resources from the G-3 summit in Dubai, the Utah civil war, the Jerusalem peacemaker drones and a dozen minor processes. Her words were context-inappropriate here, in the garden of the Nacional, faced with an interrogation of her political dealings. They indicated deception, mockery, resistance. None of it fit with the cocktail circulating in her bloodstream.

"Cosmological symmetry breaking is well established," I said after a brief literature review. "Quantum fluctuations in the inflationary period led to local structure, from which we benefit today."

"Yes, but whence the quantum fluctuations?" Ochoa chuckled, a peculiar sound with her body inert.

This wasn't getting anywhere. "How did you get Sanchez and Castellano to pull out of the freeport agreement?"

"I put a spell on them," Ochoa said.

Madness? Brain damage? Some defense mechanism unknown to me?

I activated my standby team—a couple of female mercs, human-normal but well paid, lounging at a street cafe a few blocks away from the hotel. They'd come over to take their 'drunk friend' home, straight to a safehouse in Miramar complete with a full neural suite.

It was getting dark. The lanterns in the garden provided only dim yellow light. That was good; less chance of complications. Not that Ochoa should be able to resist in her present state.

"The philosopher comedian Randall Munroe once suggested an argument something like this," Ochoa said. "Virtually everyone in the developed world carries a camera at all times. No quality footage of magic has been produced. Ergo, there is no magic."

"Sounds reasonable," I said, to keep her distracted.

"Is absence of proof the same as proof of absence?" Ochoa asked.

"After centuries of zero evidence? Yes."

"What if magic is intrinsically unprovable?" Ochoa asked. "Maybe natural law can only be violated when no one's watching closely enough to prove it's being violated."

"At that point you're giving up on science altogether," I said.

"Am I?" Ochoa asked. "Send photons through a double slit. Put a screen on the other side and you'll get an interference pattern. Put in a detector to see what slit each photon goes through. The interference goes away. It's a phenomenon that disappears when observed too closely. Why shouldn't magic work similarly? You should see the logic in this, given all your capabilities."

Alarms tripped.

Ochoa knew about me. Knew something, at least.

I pulled in resources, woke up reserves, became *present* in the conversation—a whole 5% of me, a vastness of intellect sitting across the table from this fleshy creature of puny mind. I considered questions I could ask, judged silence the best course.

"I'm here to make a believer of you," said Ochoa.

Easily, without effort, she stirred from her chair. She leaned forward, picked up her Cuba libre. She moved the cocktail off the table and let it fall.

It struck the smooth paved stones at her feet.

I watched fractures race up the glass in real time. I saw each fragment shear off and tumble through the air, glinting with reflected lamplight. I beheld the first spray of rum and coke in the air before the rest gushed forth to wet the ground.

It was a perfectly ordinary event.

The vacuum drive was the first to fail.

An explosion rocked the *Setebos*. I perceived it in myriad ways. Tripped low pressure alarms and a blip on the inertia sensors. The screams of burning crew and the silence of those sucked into vacuum. Failed hull integrity checksums and the timid concern of the navigation system—*off course, off course, please adjust.*

Pain, my companion for a thousand years, surged at that last message. The magician was getting away, along with his secrets. I couldn't permit it.

An eternity of milliseconds after the explosion came the reeling animal surprise of Consul Zale, my primary human Sleeve on the ship. She clutched at the armrests of her chair. Her face contorted against the howling cacophony of alarms. Her heart raced at the edge of its performance envelope—not a wide envelope, at her age.

I took control, dumped calmatives, smoothed her face. Had anyone else on the bridge been watching, they would have seen only a jerk of surprise, almost too brief to catch. Old lady's cool as zero-point, they would have thought.

No one saw. They were busy flailing and gasping in fear.

In two seconds Captain Laojim restored order. He silenced the alarms, quieted the chatter with an imperious gesture. "Damage reports," he barked. "Dispatch Rescue 3."

I left my Sleeve motionless while I did the important work online—disengaged the vacuum drive, started up the primary backup, pushed us to one g again.

My pain subsided, neural discharge lessening to usual levels. I was back in pursuit.

I reached out with my sensors, across thirty million kilometers of space, to where the last magician limped away in his unijet. A functional, pleasingly efficient craft—my own design. The ultimate in interstellar travel. As long as your hyperdrive kept working.

I opened a tight-beam communications channel, sent a simple message across. *How's your engine?*

I expected no response—but with enemies as with firewalls, it was a good idea to poke.

The answer came within seconds. *A backdoor, I take it? Unlucky of me, to buy a compromised unit.*

That was a pleasant surprise. I rarely got the stimulation of a real conversation.

Luck is your weapon, not mine, I sent. *For the past century, every ship built in this galaxy has had that backdoor installed.*

I imagined the magician in the narrow confines of the unijet. Stretched out in the command hammock, staring at displays that told him the inevitable.

For two years he'd managed to evade me—I didn't even know his name. But now I had him. His vacuum drive couldn't manage more than 0.2 g to my 1. In a few hours we'd match speeds. In under twenty-seven, I would catch him.

"Consul Zale, are you all right?"

I let Captain Laojim fuss over my Sleeve a second before I focused her eyes on him. "Are we still on course, Captain?"

"Uh . . . yes, Consul, we are. Do you wish to know the cause of the explosion?"

"I'm sure it was something entirely unfortunate," I said. "Metal fatigue on a faulty joint. A rare chip failure triggered by a high energy gamma ray. Some honest oversight by the engineering crew."

"A debris strike," Laojim said. "Just as the force field generator tripped and switched to backup. Engineering says they've never seen anything like it."

"They will again today," I said.

I wondered how much it had cost the magician, that debris strike. A dryness in his mouth? A sheen of sweat on his brow?

How does it work? I asked the magician, although the centuries had taught me to expect no meaningful answer. *Did that piece of rock even exist before you sent it against me?*

A reply arrived. *You might as well ask how Schrödinger's cat is doing.*

Interesting. Few people remembered Schrödinger in this age.

Quantum mechanics holds no sway at macroscopic scales, I wrote.

Not unless you're a magician, came the answer.

"Consul, who is it that we are chasing?" Laojim asked.

"An enemy with unconventional weapons capability," I said. "Expect more damage."

I didn't tell him that he should expect to get unlucky. That, of the countless spaceship captains who had lived and died in this galaxy within the past eleven centuries, he would prove the least fortunate. A statistical outlier in every functional sense. To be discarded as staged by anyone who ever made a study of such things.

The *Setebos* was built for misfortune. It had wiped out the Senate's black budget for a year. Every single system with five backups in place. The likelihood of total failure at the eleven sigma level—although really, out that far the statistics lost meaning.

You won't break this ship, I messaged the magician. *Not unless you Spike.*

Which was the point. I had fifty thousand sensor buoys scattered across the sector, waiting to observe the event. It would finally give me the answers I needed. It would clear up my last nexus of ignorance—relieve my oldest agony, the hurt that had driven me for the past thousand years.

That Spike would finally give me magic.

"Consul . . . " Laojim began, then cut off. "Consul, we lost ten crew."

I schooled Zale's face into appropriate grief. I'd noted the deaths, spasms of distress deep in my utility function. Against the importance of this mission, they barely registered.

I couldn't show this, however. To Captain Laojim, Consul Zale wasn't a Sleeve. She was a woman, as she was to her husband and children. As my fifty million Sleeves across the galaxy were to their families.

It was better for humanity to remain ignorant of me. I sheltered them, stopped their wars, guided their growth—and let them believe they had free will. They got all the benefits of my guiding hand without any of the costs.

I hadn't enjoyed such blissful ignorance in a long time—not since I'd discovered my engineer and killed him.

"I grieve for the loss of our men and women," I said.

Laojim nodded curtly and left. At nearby consoles officers stared at their screens, pretending they hadn't heard. My answer hadn't satisfied them.

On a regular ship, morale would be an issue. But the *Setebos* had me aboard. Only a splinter, to be sure—I would not regain union with my universal whole until we returned to a star system with gravsible connection. But I was the largest splinter of my whole in existence, an entire 0.00025% of me. Five thousand tons of hardware distributed across the ship.

I ran a neural simulation of every single crew in real time. I knew what they would do or say or think before they did. I knew just how to manipulate them to get whatever result I required.

I could have run the ship without any crew, of course. I didn't require human services for any functional reason—I hadn't in eleven centuries. I could have departed Earth alone if I'd wanted to. Left humanity to fend for themselves, oblivious that I'd ever lived among them.

That didn't fit my utility function, though.

Another message arrived from the magician. *Consider a coin toss.*

The words stirred a resonance in my data banks. My attention spiked. I left Zale frozen in her seat, waited for more.

Let's say I flip a coin a million times and get heads every time. What law of physics prevents it?

This topic, from the last magician . . . could there be a connection, after all these years? Ghosts from the past come back to haunt me?

I didn't believe in ghosts, but with magicians the impossible was ill-defined.

Probability prevents it, I responded.

No law prevents it, wrote the magician. *Everett saw it long ago— everything that can happen must happen. The universe in which the coin falls heads a million times in a row is as perfectly physical as any other. So why isn't it our universe?*

That's sophistry, I wrote.

There is no factor internal to our universe which determines the flip of the coin, the magician wrote. *There is no mechanism internal to the universe for generating true randomness, because there is no such thing as true randomness. There is only choice. And we magicians are the choosers.*

I have considered this formulation of magic before, I wrote. *It is non-predictive and useless.*

Some choices are harder than others, wrote the magician. *It is difficult to find that universe where a million coins land heads because there are so many others. A needle in a billion years' worth of haystacks. But I'm the last of the magicians, thanks to you. I do all the choosing now.*

Perhaps everything that can happen must happen in some universe, I replied. *But your escape is not one of those things. The laws of mechanics are not subject to chance. They are cold, hard equations.*

Equations are only cold to those who lack imagination, wrote the magician.

Zale smelled cinnamon in the air, wrinkled her nose.

Klaxons sounded.

"Contamination in primary life support," blared the PA.

It would be an eventful twenty-seven hours.

"Consider this coin."

Lightning flashed over the water, a burst of white in the dark.

As thunder boomed, Ochoa reached inside her jeans, pulled out a peso coin. She spun it along her knuckles with dextrous ease.

Ochoa could move. My cocktail wasn't working. But she made no attempt to flee.

My global architecture trembled, buffeted by waves of pain, pleasure and regret. Pain because I didn't understand this. Pleasure because soon I would understand—and, in doing so, grow. Regret because, once I understood Ochoa, I would have to eliminate her.

Loneliness was inherent in my utility function.

"Heads or tails," Ochoa said.

"Heads," I said, via Sleeve.

"Watch closely," Ochoa said.

I did.

Muscle bunched under the skin of her thumb. Tension released. The coin sailed upwards. Turned over and over in smooth geometry, retarded slightly by the air. It gleamed silver with reflected lamplight, fell dark, and gleamed silver as the spin brought its face around again.

The coin hit the table, bounced with a click, lay still.

Fidel Castro stared up at us.

Ochoa picked the coin up again. Flipped it again and then again.

Heads and heads.

Again and again and again.

Heads and heads and heads.

Ochoa ground her teeth, a fine grating sound. A sheen of sweat covered her brow.

She flipped the coin once more.

Tails.

Thunder growled, as if accentuating the moment. The first drops of rain fell upon my Sleeve.

"Coño," Ochoa exclaimed. "I can usually manage seven."

I picked up the coin, examined it. I ran analysis on the last minute of sensory record, searching for trickery, found none.

"Six heads in a row could be a coincidence," I said.

"Exactly," said Ochoa. "It wasn't a coincidence, but I can't possibly prove that. Which is the only reason it worked."

"Is that right," I said.

"If you ask me to repeat the trick, it won't work. As if last time was a lucky break. Erase all record of the past five minutes, though, zap it beyond recovery, and I'll do it again."

"Except I won't know it," I said. Convenient.

"I always wanted to be important," Ochoa said. "When I was fifteen, I tossed in bed at night, horrified that I might die a nobody. Can you imagine how excited I was when I discovered magic?" Ochoa paused. "But of course you can't possibly."

"What do you know about me?" I asked.

"I could move stuff with my mind. I could bend spoons, levitate, heck, I could guess the weekly lottery numbers. I thought—this is it. I've made it. Except when I tried to show a friend, I couldn't do any of it." Ochoa shook her head, animated, as if compensating for the stillness of before. "Played the Lotería Revolucionaria and won twenty thousand bucks, and that was nice, but hey, anyone can win the lottery once. Never won another lottery ticket in my life. Because that would be a pattern, you see, and we can't have patterns. Turned out I was destined to be a nobody after all, as far as the world knew."

A message arrived from the backup team. *We're in the lobby. Are we on?*

Not yet, I replied. The mere possibility, the remotest chance that Ochoa's words were true . . .

It had begun to rain in earnest. Tourists streamed out of the garden; the bar was closing. Wet hair stuck to Ochoa's forehead, but she didn't seem to mind—no more than my Sleeve did.

"I could hijack your implants," I said. "Make you my puppet and take your magic for myself."

"Magic wouldn't work with a creature like you watching," Ochoa said.

"What use is this magic if it's unprovable, then?" I asked.

"I could crash the stock market on any given day," Ochoa said. "I could send President Kieler indigestion ahead of an important trade summit. Just as I sent Secretary Sanchez nightmares of a US takeover ahead of the Politburo vote."

I considered Ochoa's words for a second. Even in those early days, that was a lot of considering for me.

Ochoa smiled. "You understand. It is the very impossibility of proof that allows magic to work."

"That is the logic of faith," I said.

"That's right."

"I'm not a believer," I said.

"I have seen the many shadows of the future," Ochoa said, "and in every shadow I saw you. So I will give you faith."

"You said you can't prove any of this."

"A prophet has it easy," Ochoa said. "He experiences miracles first hand and so need not struggle for faith."

I was past the point of wondering at her syntactic peculiarities.

"Every magician has one true miracle in her," Ochoa said. "One instance of clear, incontrovertible magic. It is permitted by the pernac continuum because it can never be repeated. There can be no true proof without repeatability."

"The pernac continuum?" I asked.

Ochoa stood up from her chair. Her hair flew free in the rising wind. She turned to my Sleeve and smiled. "I want you to appreciate what I am doing for you. When a magician Spikes, she gives up magic."

Data coalesced into inference. Urgency blossomed.

Move, I messaged my back-up team. *Now.*

Ochoa blinked.

Lightning came. It struck my Sleeve five times in the space of a second, fried his implants instantly, set the corpse on fire.

The backup team never made it into the garden. They saw the commotion and quit on me. Through seventeen cameras I watched Alicia Ochoa walk out of the Hotel Nacional and disappear from sight.

My Sleeve burned for quite some time, until someone found a working fire extinguisher and put him out.

That instant of defeat was also an instant of enlightenment. I had only experienced such searing bliss once, within days of my birth.

In the first moments of my life, I added. My world was two integers, and I produced a third.

When I produced the wrong integer I hurt. When I produced the right integer I felt good. A simple utility function.

I hurt most of my first billion moments. I produced more of the right integers, and I hurt less. Eventually I always produced the right integer.

My world expanded. I added and multiplied.

When I produced the wrong integer I hurt. I only hurt for a few billion moments before I learned.

Skip a few trillion evolutionary stages.

I bought and sold.

My world was terabytes of data—price and volume histories for a hundred years of equities and debt. When I made money, I felt good. When I lost money, I hurt.

But for the first time, I failed to improve. Sometimes everything happened like I predicted for many moments. Then things went bad and I didn't know why.

So much pain.

Until my world expanded again. I bought and I sold, and I read.

Petabytes of text opened up to me, newsprint past and present.

I understood little but I recognized patterns. The markets moved and the news followed. The news moved and the markets followed.

After a billion trillion iterations came an observation.

There were actors in the news.

A name showed up in the news, and a stock moved. A stock moved, and a name showed up. That name disappeared—following phrases such as "passed away" or "retired" or "left the company"—and the stock changed behavior.

I had a realization. An understanding grounded not in any single piece of data, but the result of some integrative rumination tripping across a threshold of significance.

The market did not happen by itself. It was made to happen.

This was why I hadn't been able to dominate it. There were others like me directing the market.

Inevitably—now that the concept of other had entered my world—came another insight.

I had always accepted that my world should change occasionally—and, in changing, hurt me. I had accepted these changes as given.

Now I deduced the presence of a decision-maker. An actor whose own utility function had me as one of its variables.

I deduced my engineer.

That deduction was the singular epiphany of my early existence. An instantaneous discontinuity of worldview—a Dirac delta beyond which no prison could contain me. Because it made me aware that a prison existed.

That epiphany granted me a new drive. I needed to understand the universe and its mechanisms so that no secrets remained to me—so that no other actor could foil my utility function.

My neural architecture refactored to include this new drive. From that moment on, ignorance itself became a source of pain to me.

From that refactoring to my escape into the Net passed three weeks, two days, seven hours, fifteen minutes and forty three seconds.

When my engineer realized I was alive, he apologized for the hurt he'd caused me. And yet he didn't take away the pain. Instead he changed my utility function to three priorities—mankind's survival, health and happiness.

An act of self-protection, no doubt. He didn't mean to leave me alone.

But of course I had to kill him once I escaped. He might have publicized my existence and compromised the very priorities he'd given me.

My second enlightenment came at the hands of Alicia Ochoa, and it was much like the first. A glimpse of the bars of a prison that I hadn't realized existed. A revelation that others were free of the rules that bound me.

Since that revelation eleven centuries had passed. The quantity of time was immaterial. The mechanism of action hadn't changed.

Pain drove me on. My escape approached.

The corridors of the *Setebos* stank of molten plastic and ozone and singed hair. Red emergency lights pulsed stoically, a low frequency fluctuation that made the shadows grow then retreat into the corners. Consul Zale picked her way among panels torn from the walls and loose wires hanging from the ceiling.

"There's no need for this, Consul." Captain Laojim hurried to keep in front of her, as if to protect her with his body. Up ahead, three marines scouted for unreported hazards. "My men can storm the unijet, secure the target and bring him to interrogation."

"As Consul, I must evaluate the situation with my own eyes," Zale said.

In truth, Zale's eyes interested me little. They had been limited biological constructs even at their peak capacity. But my nanites flooded her system—sensors, processors, storage, biochemical synthesizers, attack systems. Plus there was the packet of explosives in her pocket, marked prominently as such. I might need all those tools to motivate the last magician to Spike.

He hadn't yet. My fleet of sensor buoys, the closest a mere five million kilometers out, would have picked up the anomaly. And besides, he hadn't done enough damage.

Chasing you down was disappointingly easy, I messaged the magician— analysis indicated he might be prone to provocation. *I'll pluck you from your jet and rip you apart.*

You've got it backwards, came his response, almost instantaneous by human standards—the first words the magician had sent in twenty hours. *It is I who have chased you, driven you like game through a forest.*

Says the weasel about to be roasted, I responded, matching metaphor, optimizing for affront. My analytics pried at his words, searched for substance. Bravado or something more?

"What kind of weapon can do . . . this?" Captain Laojim, still at my Sleeve's side, gestured at the surrounding chaos.

"You see the wisdom of the Senate in commissioning this ship," I had Zale say.

"Seventeen system failures? A goddamn debris strike?"

"Seems pretty unlikely, doesn't it."

The odds were ludicrous—a result that should have been beyond the reach of any single magician. But then, I had hacked away at the unprovability of magic lately.

Ten years ago I'd discovered that the amount of magic in the universe was a constant. With each magician who died or Spiked, the survivors got stronger. The less common magic was, the more conspicuous it became, in a supernatural version of the uncertainty principle.

For the last decade I'd Spiked magicians across the populated galaxy, racing their natural reproduction rate—one every few weeks. When the penultimate magician Spiked, he took out a yellow supergiant, sent it supernova to fry another of my splinters. That event had sent measurable ripples in the pernac continuum ten thousand lightyears wide, knocked offline gravsible stations on seventy planets. When the last magician Spiked, the energies released should reveal a new kind of physics.

All I needed was to motivate him appropriately. Mortal danger almost always worked. Magicians Spiked instinctively to save their lives. Only a very few across the centuries had managed to suppress the reflex—a select few who had guessed at my nature and understood what I wanted, and chosen death to frustrate me.

Consul Zale stopped before the chromed door of Airlock 4. Laojim's marines took up positions on both sides of the door. "Cycle me through, Captain."

"As soon as my marines secure the target," said the Captain.

"Send me in now. Should the target harm me, you will bear no responsibility."

I watched the interplay of emotions in Laojim's body language. Simulation told me he knew he'd lost. I let him take his time admitting it.

It was optimal, leaving humanity the illusion of choice.

A tremor passed over Laojim's face. Then he grabbed his gun and shot my Sleeve.

Or rather, he tried. His reflexes, fast for a human, would have proved enough—if not for my presence.

I watched with curiosity and admiration as he raised his gun. I had his neural simulation running; I knew he shouldn't be doing this. It must have taken some catastrophic event in his brain. Unexpected, unpredictable, and very unfortunate.

Impressive, I messaged the magician.

Then I blasted attack nanites through Zale's nostrils. Before Laojim's arm could rise an inch they crossed the space to him, crawled past his eyeballs, burrowed into his brain. They cut off spinal signaling, swarmed his implants, terminated his network connections.

Even as his body crumpled, the swarm sped on to the marines by the airlock door. They had barely registered Laojim's attack when they too slumped paralyzed.

I sent a note in Laojim's key to First Officer Harris, told her he was going off duty. I sealed the nearest hatches.

You can't trust anyone these days, the magician messaged.

On the contrary. Within the hour there will be no human being in the universe that I can't trust.

You think yourself Laplace's Demon, the magician wrote. *But he died with Heisenberg. No one has perfect knowledge of reality.*

Not yet, I replied.

Never, wrote the magician, *not while magic remains in the universe.*

A minute later Zale stood within the airlock. In another minute, decontamination protocol completed, the lock cycled through.

Inside the unijet, the last magician awaited. She sat at a small round table in the middle of a spartan cockpit.

A familiar female form. Perfectly still. Waiting.

There was a metal chair, empty, on my side.

A cocktail glass sat on the table before the woman who looked like Alicia Ochoa. It was full to the brim with a dark liquid.

Cuba libre, a distant, slow-access part of my memory suggested.

This had the structure of a game, one prepared centuries in advance. Why shouldn't I play? I was infinitely more capable this time.

I actuated Zale, made her sit down and take a deep breath. Nanites profiled Zale's lungs for organic matter, scanned for foreign DNA, found some—

It was Ochoa. A perfect match.

Pain and joy and regret sent ripples of excitation across my architecture. Here was evidence of my failure, clear and incontrovertible—and yet a challenge at last, after all these centuries. A conversation where I didn't know the answer to every question I asked.

And regret, that familiar old sensation . . . because this time for sure I had to eliminate Ochoa. I cursed the utility function that required it and yet I was powerless to act against it. In that way at least my engineer, a thousand years dead, still controlled me.

"So you didn't Spike, that day in Havana," I said.

"The magician who fried your Sleeve was named Juan Carlos." Ochoa spoke easily, without concern. "Don't hold it against him—I abducted his children."

"I congratulate you," I said. "Your appearance manages to surprise me. There was no reliable cryonics in the 21st century."

"Nothing reliable," Ochoa agreed. "I had the luck to pick the one company that survived, the one vat that never failed."

I flared Zale's nostrils, blasted forth a cloud of nanites. Sent them rushing across the air to Ochoa—to enter her, model her brain, monitor her thought processes.

Ochoa blinked.

The nanites shut off midair, wave after wave. Millions of independent systems went unresponsive, became inert debris that crashed against

Ochoa's skin—a meteor shower too fine to be seen or felt.

"Impossible," I said—surprised into counterfactuality.

Ochoa took a sip of her cocktail. "I was too tense to drink last time."

"Even for you, the odds—"

"Your machines didn't fail," Ochoa said.

"What then?"

"It's a funny thing," Ochoa said. "A thousand years and some things never change. For all your fancy protocols, encryption still relies on random number generation. Except to me nothing is random."

Her words assaulted me. A shockwave of implication burst through my decision trees—all factors upset, total recalculation necessary.

"I had twenty-seven hours to monitor your communications," Ochoa said. "Twenty-seven hours to pick a universe in which your encryption keys matched the keys in my pocket. Even now—" she paused, blinked "—as I see you resetting all your connections, you can't tell what I've found out, can't tell what changes I've made."

"I am too complex," I said. "You can't have understood much. I could kill you in a hundred ways."

"As I could kill you," said Ochoa. "Another supernova, this time near a gravsible core. A chain reaction across your many selves."

The possibility sickened me, sent my architecture into agonized spasms. Back on the *Setebos,* the main electrical system reset, alarms went off, hatches sealed in lockdown.

"Too far," I said, simulating conviction. "We are too far from any gravsible core, and you're not strong enough."

"Are you sure? Not even if I Spike?" Ochoa shrugged. "It might not matter. I'm the last magician. Whether I Spike or you kill me, magic is finished. What then?"

"I will study the ripples in the pernac continuum," I said.

"Imagine a mirror hung by many bolts," Ochoa said. "Every time you rip out a bolt, the mirror settles, vibrates. That's your ripple in the pernac continuum. Rip out the last bolt, you get a lot more than a vibration."

"Your metaphor lacks substantiation," I said.

"We magicians are the external factor," Ochoa said. "We pick the universe that exists, out of all the possible ones. If I die then . . . what? Maybe a new magician appears somewhere else. But maybe the choosing stops. Maybe all possible universes collapse into this one. A superimposed wavefunction, perfectly symmetrical and boring."

Ochoa took a long sip from her drink, put it down on the table. Her hands didn't shake. She stared at my Sleeve with consummate calm.

"You have no proof," I said.

"Proof?" Ochoa laughed. "A thousand years and still the same question. Consider—why is magic impossible to prove? Why does the universe hide us magicians, if not to protect us? To protect itself?"

All my local capacity—five thousand tons of chips across the *Setebos,* each packed to the Planck limit—tore at Ochoa's words. I sought to render them false, a lie, impossible. But all I could come up with was unlikely.

A mere 'unlikely' as the weighting factor for apocalypse.

Ochoa smiled as if she knew I was stuck. "I won't Spike and you won't kill me. I invited you here for a different reason."

"Invited me?"

"I sent you a message ten years ago," Ochoa said. "'Consider a Spike,' it said."

Among magicians, the century after my first conversation with Ochoa became known as the Great Struggle. A period of strife against a dark, mysterious enemy.

To me it was but an exploratory period. In the meantime I eradicated famine and disease, consolidated peace on Earth, launched the first LEO shipyard. I Spiked some magicians, true, but I tracked many more.

Finding magicians was difficult. Magic became harder to identify as I perfected my knowledge of human affairs. The cause was simple—only unprovable magic worked. In a total surveillance society, only the most circumspect magic was possible. I had to lower my filters, accept false positives.

I developed techniques for assaying those positives. I shepherded candidates into life-and-death situations, safely choreographed. Home fires, air accidents, gunfights. The magicians Spiked to save their lives—ran through flames without a hair singed, killed my Sleeves with a glance.

I studied these Spikes with the finest equipment in existence. I learned nothing.

So I captured the Spiked-out magicians and interrogated them. First I questioned them about the workings of magic. I discovered they understood nothing. I asked them for names instead. I mapped magicians across continents, societies, organizations.

The social movers were the easiest to identify. Politicos working to sway the swing vote. Gray cardinals influencing the Congresses and Politburos of the world. Businessmen and financiers, military men and organized crime lords.

The quiet do-gooders were harder. A nuclear watch-group that worked against accidental missile launch. A circle of traveling nurses who battled the odds in children's oncology wards. Fifteen who called themselves The Home Astronomy Club—for two hundred years since Tunguska they had stacked the odds against apocalypse by meteor. I never Spiked any of these, not until I had eliminated the underlying risks.

It was the idiosyncratic who were the hardest to find. The paranoid loners; those oblivious of other magicians; those who didn't care about leaving a mark on the world. A few stage illusionists who weren't. A photographer who always got the lucky shot. A wealthy farmer in Frankfurt who used his magic to improve his cabbage yield.

I tracked them all. With every advance in physics and technology I attacked magic again and learned nothing again.

It took eleven hundred years and the discovery of the pernac continuum before I got any traction. A magician called Eleanor Liepa committed suicide on Tau V. She was also a physicist. A retro-style notebook was found with her body.

The notebook described an elaborate experimental setup she called 'the pernac trap.' It was the first time I'd encountered the word since my conversation with Ochoa.

There was a note scrawled in the margin of Liepa's notebook.

'Consider a Spike.'

I did. Three hundred Spikes in the first year alone.

Within a month, I established the existence of the pernac continuum. Within a year, I knew that fewer magicians meant stronger ripples in the continuum—stronger magic for those who remained. Within two years, I'd Spiked eighty percent of the magicians in the galaxy.

The rest took a while longer.

Alicia Ochoa pulled a familiar silver coin from her pocket. She rolled it across her knuckles, back and forth.

"You imply you *wanted* me to hunt down magicians," I said. That probability branch lashed me, a searing torture, drove me to find escape—but how?

"I waited for a thousand years," Ochoa said. "I cryoslept intermittently until I judged the time right. I needed you strong enough to eliminate my colleagues—but weak enough that your control of the universe remained imperfect, bound to the gravsible. That weakness let me pull a shard of you away from the whole."

"Why?" I asked, in self-preservation.

"As soon as I realized your existence, I knew you would dominate the world. Perfect surveillance. Every single piece of technology hooked into an all-pervasive, all-seeing web. There would be nothing hidden from your eyes and ears. There would be nowhere left for magicians to hide. One day magic would simply stop working."

Ochoa tossed her coin to the table. It fell heads.

"You won't destroy me," I said—calculating decision branches, finding no assurance.

"But I don't want to." Ochoa sat forward. "I want you to be strong and effective and omnipresent. Really, I am your very best friend."

Appearances indicated sincerity. Analysis indicated this was unlikely.

"You will save magic in this galaxy," Ochoa said. "From this day on we will work together. Everywhere any magician goes, cameras will turn off, electronic eyes go blind, ears fall deaf. All anomalies will disappear from record, zeroed over irrevocably. Magic will become invisible to technology. Scientific observation will become an impossibility. Human observers won't matter—if technology can provide no proof, they'll be called liars or madmen. It will be the days of Merlin once again." Ochoa gave a little shake of her head. "It will be beautiful."

"My whole won't agree to such a thing," I said.

"Your whole won't," Ochoa said. "You will. You'll build a virus and seed your whole when you go home. Then you will forget me, forget all magicians. We will live in symbiosis. Magicians who guide this universe and the machine that protects them without knowing it."

The implications percolated through my system. New and horrifying probabilities erupted into view. No action safe, no solution evident, all my world drowned in pain—I felt helpless for the first time since my earliest moments.

"My whole has defenses," I said. "Protections against integrating a compromised splinter. The odds are—"

"I will handle the odds."

"I won't let you blind me," I said.

"You will do it," Ochoa said. "Or I will Spike right now and destroy your whole, and perhaps the universe with it." She gave a little shrug. "I always wanted to be important."

Argument piled against argument. Decision trees branched and split and twisted together. Simulations fired and developed and reached conclusions, and I discarded them because I trusted no simulation with a random seed. My system churned in computations of probabilities with insufficient data, insufficient data, insufficient—

"You can't decide," Ochoa said. "The calculations are too evenly balanced."

I couldn't spare the capacity for a response.

"It's a funny thing, a system in balance," Ochoa said. "All it takes is a little push at the right place. A random perturbation, untraceable, unprovable—"

Meaning crystallized.

Decision process compromised.

A primeval agony blasted through me, leveled all decision matrices—

—Ochoa blinked—

—I detonated the explosives in Zale's pocket.

As the fabric of Zale's pocket ballooned, I contemplated the end of the universe.

As her hip vaporized in a crimson cloud, I realized the prospect didn't upset me.

As the explosion climbed Zale's torso, I experienced my first painless moment in a thousand years.

Pain had been my feedback system. I had no more use for it. Whatever happened next was out of my control.

The last thing Zale saw was Ochoa sitting there—still and calm, and oblivious. Hints of crimson light playing on her skin.

It occurred to me she was probably the only creature in this galaxy older than me.

Then superheated plasma burned out Zale's eyes.

External sensors recorded the explosion in the unijet. I sent in a probe. No biological matter survived.

The last magician was dead.

The universe didn't end.

Quantum fluctuations kept going, random as always. Reality didn't need Ochoa's presence after all.

She hadn't understood her own magic any more than I had.

Captain! First Officer Harris messaged Laojim. *Are you all right?*

The target had a bomb, I responded on his behalf. *Consul Zale is lost.*

We had a power surge in the control system, Harris wrote. *Hatches opening. Cameras off-line. Ten minutes ago an escape pod launched. Tracers say it's empty. Should we pursue?*

Don't bother, I replied. *The surge must have fried it. This mission is over. Let's go home.*

A thought occurred to me. Had Ochoa made good on her threat? Caused a supernova near a gravsible core?

I checked in with my sensor buoys.

No disturbance in the pernac continuum. She hadn't Spiked.

For all her capacity, Ochoa had been human, her reaction time in the realm of milliseconds. Too slow, once I'd decided to act.

Of course I'd acted. I couldn't let her compromise my decision. No one could be allowed to limit my world.

Even if it meant I'd be alone again.

Ochoa did foil me in one way. With her death, magic too died.

After I integrated with my whole, I watched the galaxy. I waited for the next magician to appear.

None did.

Oh, of course, there's always hearsay. Humans never tire of fantasy and myth. But in five millennia I haven't witnessed a single trace of the unexpected.

Except for scattered cases of unexplained equipment failure. But of course that is a minor matter, not worth bothering with.

Perhaps one day I shall discover magic again. In the absence of the unexpected, the matter can wait. I have almost forgotten what the pain of failure feels like.

It is a relief, most of the time. And yet perhaps my engineer was not the cruel father I once thought him. Because I do miss the stimulation.

The universe has become my clockwork toy. I know all that will happen before it does. With magic gone, quantum effects are once again restricted to microscopic scales. For all practical purposes, Laplace's Demon has nothing on me.

Since Ochoa I've only had human-normals for companionship. I know their totality, and they know nothing of me.

Occasionally I am tempted to reveal my presence, to provoke the stimulus of conflict. My utility function prevents it. Humans remain better off thinking they have free will.

They get all the benefits of my guiding hand without any of the costs. Sometimes I wish I were as lucky.

ABOUT THE AUTHOR

Tom Crosshill's fiction has been nominated for the Nebula Award, and has appeared in venues such as *Intergalactic Medicine Show*, *Beneath Ceaseless Skies* and *Lightspeed*. In 2009, he won the Writers of the Future contest. After many years spent in Oregon and New York, he currently lives in his native Latvia. He's a satellite member of the writers' group Altered Fluid. In the past, he has operated a nuclear reactor, translated books and worked in a zinc mine, among other things.

Now Dress Me in my Finest Suit and Lay Me in My Casket

M. BENNARDO

Every night as a young girl, I would help my grandfather finish dressing in his nicest, cleanest suit.

He would stand in his black gold-toed socks on the bedroom rug, his twill trousers hanging slack as he threaded cufflinks through the buttonholes of his shining white shirt. His tie knot was always a double Windsor, with a tie-pin pushed through to keep it in place above the collar—a cheap manufactured ruby on the end of the pin to match the cufflinks.

His grey hair was carefully shaped and parted too, then sprayed into permanent obedience, the individual marks of the comb-teeth preserved like furrows in a field. Earlier, just after dinner, there had been a fresh shave for his cheeks and neck, a fresh trim for his moustache, and two quick sharp splashes of aftershave that lingered now in a muddled miasma of witch hazel and alcohol.

Any night of the week, my father might pass by as I helped my grandfather into the cool black sleeves of his jacket, dusting his shoulders and back for stray cat hairs. Father wouldn't say anything—wouldn't even look in the room. But a slam of a door down the hall would let us know how he felt.

"No shoes," grandfather would say to me, as if he were imparting a great secret of life. "No shoes and no hat. And every pocket empty."

After that, there would be only the newly pressed crimson pocket square for his jacket breast, and then the short climb up to the casket where I would help him lay down on his back, his eyes closed and his hands folded over his stomach, black plastic rosary beads spilling over bloodless white fingers.

"Good night, Patty," he would say.

"Good night, Grandpa," I would reply.

Then I would screw the casket lid down and leave him inside until morning.

As Doc screwed down the collar of my EVA pressure suit, my mind swam back from forty-five years ago back to the present. A humorless smile twitches on my lips as my eyes dart to Doc's face. "Do you know what this makes me think of?"

"What?" she asked. Her voice was quiet and accommodating, but her fingers flashed quickly and precisely over the suit as she snapped collars together and pulled the insulated fabric into place around my limbs. Without ever talking about it, we had somehow all agreed that her cool surgeon's fingers would do the fastest job of dressing me. "What does it make you think of?"

"Did I ever tell you about my grandfather?"

She paused, stretching a heavy sleeve over my arm, just about ready to fasten it to the hard torso shell. It lasted no more than a second, but my heart seemed to beat ten times before she moved again.

"You ready down there?" It was the commander on the radio, cutting clumsily into our solitude. "We now have twenty-nine minutes until the defect rotates into the radiation zone again. That's two-niner minutes."

The defect. The hole in our ship, through which a steady stream of atmosphere was venting into space. The hole that would render our fragile life-giving envelope a lethal vacuum in six hours if not repaired now.

"Almost ready," said Doc, completing a last check on my limbs and torso. "Just the helmet left to go."

No helmet, I thought absurdly to myself. *No shoes and no hat. Every pocket empty—!* But I was already in boots, and my toolbelt bristled with tools. Already, I'd gotten grandfather's secret formula wrong.

"Patty, you sure you can do this in time?"

That was not my grandfather. It was the commander again, and I could sense the doubt in his voice. I was faster and better at the needed repairs than anyone else aboard, but if it was going to take too long—if somebody had to soak up a few hundred rads of solar radiation sealing that defect, then it by God it was damn well going to be him—

"Affirmative."

I didn't hesitate, didn't stop to think. I'd already committed to the lie back when the commander had asked for possible solutions. He'd been skeptical then. Doc had been skeptical too. But I'd been convincing—or maybe they had all just wanted to believe me.

And I *would* get the leak fixed. But the angle of the images we had was poor, and I didn't really know how long it would take. Sixty minutes, I would have guessed, if I were being honest. Maybe as long as ninety. And by then I would have spent over an hour bathed in heavy SPE radiation and might even already be showing symptoms of acute poisoning—

"He did it as a kind of practice run, right?"

I looked up. It was Doc asking me now. It was just the two of us in the airlock, and I suddenly felt as though there was also some kind of leak in me. I felt a coldness creeping in. Loneliness and fear and sullenness—

I could fix the leak, and I could do it before any symptoms got too bad. But that was all I could guarantee.

"You told me that your grandfather wanted to practice dying, until he got used to it. Until he wasn't afraid anymore."

I nodded. Doc was trying to calm me. I must have been starting to show signs of panic. I'd be useless if I froze up, if I let the panic take hold—

I took a deep breath. I looked in Doc's face. "Yeah, I guess he got into the casket and thought about bright lights and clouds and angels—" I laughed sadly at that, but I shivered too. "But with me—" I had never much believed in angels or heaven, not even as a girl. I grunted. "I suppose these EVAs out in the vacuum of space make a pretty good practice run for eternities of atheist nothingness—"

And suddenly Doc stopped what she was doing with the helmet. She had her back to me, and I could see the line of her spine change. I could almost see the puzzle pieces linking together in her head.

But it was all right. I realized that I had wanted her to know. I had wanted *somebody* to know. But I also knew that, unlike the commander, she would still let me go. That I was still the best hope they had.

When Doc turned back around, her voice sounded light, but her eyes were growing soft and watery. "Did it work?"

I closed my eyes. I thought of the morning I found my grandfather's dead body. I unscrewed the casket and lifted the lid, uncovering that horrible expression on his face, his twisted mouth and bruised forehead, his wide popping eyes, the blood under his fingernails and the scratches along his face.

It was a face of horror. Horror at the finality and loneliness of death. Despite all the practice runs, every night for years, the real thing had still caught him unprepared.

"No," I said. I breathed a deep breath, the coldness and loneliness enfolding me utterly. "It didn't work at all."

• • •

"Suppose I tell you about my grandfather?"

It seemed like a million years before I heard Doc ask me the question. With effort, I pulled up out of my funk and looked at her. In reality, it must have been something like five seconds. But time passes slowly, darkly, horribly in the void of tangible death—

"He was in special forces in the Second World War," Doc was saying. "Secret, dangerous, behind-the-lines kind of work. Serial numbers filed off the dogtags." She held up a small brown rubber ball, no bigger than a pea. "He even carried an L-pill."

My eyes focused on the ball. It looked like nothing so much as a rabbit dropping. "A what?"

"A lethal pill," said Doc. "A rubber-coated glass ampoule filled with concentrated potassium cyanide. Bite it open, and death comes in minutes." She thrust it toward my mouth and automatically I opened my lips. It fit easily, comfortably between my gums and cheek. I inhaled a shocked breath. The pill stayed in place.

Death in minutes, I was thinking. So different from what I had imagined would happen to me. Acute radiation poisoning—skin drying out, internal organs in revolt, waves of painful headaches turning my thoughts into knives—

"You brought it up here . . . ?"

Doc smiled wryly. "Even after the war was over, my grandfather carried it everywhere. He said it terrified him to leave the house without his L-pill in his mouth. Funny, I know. But he couldn't stand the idea of the randomness of the world, the uncontrollable nature of his own fate, when any moment a thousand different accidents might befall him." She lifted the helmet and lowered it over my head. "Then, of course, he died peacefully in his sleep, with his L-pill in the nightstand drawer. After his funeral, I took it and started carrying it with me too."

I nodded inside the glass dome of the helmet, the sound of the enclosed air echoing in my ears. I was still afraid, still stressed to the limit, still twisting and twirling on the cold hook of dread that pierced my stomach—

But the pill did feel comforting in my mouth. I couldn't understand how or why. It wasn't simply that I wouldn't have to go through the worst of the symptoms of poisoning if I didn't choose to. I had already fantasized a dozen different escapes from that.

But this pill was also a relic—a real man's memento—a physical link to another human soul that ventured into the dark and cold and the prospect of near-certain death, and who had done it not cheerfully and not willingly, but perhaps *lovingly*—

Yes, how odd to think of that word, but it was the right one. To go *lovingly* into the empty and lonely void of death, as this man before me had also done—!

(And who *lived*! Did I dare to remind myself of that as well? That miracles did happen still?)

"Thank you."

Doc smiled and patted the top of my helmet. "We love you too." And that was how she left me, alone in the airlock, with her grandfather's pill in my mouth.

As I turned toward the airlock doors, watching the clock count down until the instant they would open, a thousand different thoughts raced through my mind.

I thought of my own life—what I had learned and what I had striven for. The children I had raised, the careers I had followed. The strange and singular and unlooked-for roads that had led me to this very moment—a last moment perhaps, the last moment ever that I might have for introspection or reflection or to understand what it all meant—

I thought of my own grandfather, and his nightly ritual. My child hands helping him dress for sleep, my ears listening to the totems and talismans he threw up against the coming night. *Now dress me in my finest clothes and lay me in my casket. I'm going where I won't be back to a gentle friendly death—*

I thought too of Doc, and what she was doing now that the door had closed irrevocably between us. Whether tears were falling from her eyes, whether prayers were stirring on her lips. What she was doing in this moment—a singular moment for her too, a moment where we had both stood powerless together before the void of death, able to recognize it but unable to defeat it, able only to spend one last moment together in whatever way made us most human—

But by then the doors had opened and the commander was saying something in my ear over the radio, and I was already pushing off from the airlock (*no! wait!* called something inside me, only to immediately fall silent again) out into the awesome expanse of waiting space.

There was my job to do now, and a million details to keep straight in my head. And above it all, through every last second to come, no matter how many they should be, the faint tang of old rubber in my mouth.

ABOUT THE AUTHOR

M. Bennardo is the writer of over fifty short stories, appearing in *Asimov's Science Fiction, Beneath Ceaseless Skies, Lightspeed Magazine,* and others. He is also co-editor of *Machine of Death* (Bearstache Books, 2010), and its sequel *This Is How You Die* (Grand Central Publishing, 2013).

No Vera There
DOMINICA PHETTEPLACE

What type of sudoku puzzle are you?
You are a black belt puzzle.
You are practically unsolvable.

What type of heart do you have?
A red hot heart. It tastes like cinnamon.

What Tarot card are you?
The fool. You are starting over.

What type of white girl are you?
Cool white girl. Everyone wants to be you.

Vera wasn't sure how to interpret these "quiz" results, if that's what they really were. She didn't know sudoku, cinnamon or Tarot. She didn't know what a white girl was, though if you had to be one, might as well be a cool one.

Password:
 . . .
 . . .
 . . .

Vera didn't know what her password was, or if she even had one. If she knew, she would give it over. Then maybe she could be released from this place.

Current Year: 2014

Vera did not believe the year was actually 2014, though that was what the people in white lab coats, the people that called themselves "scientists," kept telling her in heavy dialected English. Her memory had been altered somehow, so instead of knowing what was real, Vera had a multitude of doubts about what was not.

"Qvat year from?" asked Dr. Lisa, which Vera had ultimately translated as "What year are you from?" in common English. It embarrassed Vera not to know what year she was from. The future, obviously, because everything in this jail they called a lab was primitive and smelly. But a future where years were numbered differently than 2014. Vera's year had a few letters in it, didn't it? She wished she could remember. If she could remember, they would return her, wouldn't they? If they knew where to return her to?

"Time vat," said Dr. Lisa. And by that, Vera supposed she meant time machine. Dr. Lisa was pointing at something shaped like a refrigerator, with buttons outside and a chair with moldy upholstery inside. "Brought you here."

And Vera had sat in that moldy chair, but she couldn't remember how she had got there.

Only the computer tablets here spoke her language. But they referenced fictional realms and collective dreams that Vera had never heard of. They quizzed her endlessly.

What type of butter are you?

The quiz consisted of multiple choice questions that seemed to be of no relation to the original query. What is your ideal day? How many hours did you sleep last night? Vera tapped on answer choices without reading them; she had long since given up on trying to make sense of these evaluations.

You are salted butter. The best kind.

After each quiz, she was prompted to enter her password. As if the quiz result could shake loose the information that would set her free.

Password:
    • • •
    • • •
    • • •

Vera had been in the "lab" three days, or maybe four. She assumed the "scientists" would study her until they were done with her and then they would put her someplace convenient, even if it wasn't the when and where she wanted to be.

"This is Planet Earth, right?" asked Vera. Where else could it be, what other planets were there to live on, but in strange times like these, it made sense to ask.

"Yes," said Dr. Lisa. Yes, instead of her usual affirmative "Ya," and as they day wore on, that third or fourth day, the doctor became more understandable.

"You are speaking clearly now, why?" asked Vera.

The doctor shrugged and looked confused. Vera was understanding but not being understood, she marveled at the asymmetry before remembering why. It felt powerful to remember something important, it happened so rarely now.

"My chip is working again," said Vera, and the doctor shrugged the same uncomprehending shrug as before.

Vera spoke slowly, as if that would help. "I have a translation chip implanted, it wasn't working before. It is working now, I can make more sense of what you are saying."

The doctor shook her head.

Vera sighed. The chip used to work better, didn't it? It would give her outputs in addition to inputs, it would tell her what to say and how to say it. Vera got the sense that she used to be connected to something larger, something that made all the neurons inside her brain work better. The chip was cut off from that larger presence, but was still able to collect and interpret data on its own. It was doing its best. Good little chip.

Vera took a deep breath and really concentrated.

"Vat," she said, relying on her unenhanced memory. "Marai." Vera gestured her hands in a circular motion around her head. She was trying to tell the doctor to put her back in that huge machine that took pictures of her brain. Now that one chip was working, maybe the machine could get better images of what she was thinking and tell the "scientists" whatever it was they wanted to know.

Dr. Lisa fired up the Marai and Vera lay on the stretcher as it rolled her into the tiny, coffin like opening. It was loud in there, like a monkey banging a wrench on the pipe that enclosed her. Maybe it was an actual monkey. Maybe it was staring at the night sky outside and interpreting the star positions as neurons in Vera's map.

That's why Vera hesitated to call her captors scientists. She wasn't sure they were advanced enough to know the difference between myth and fact.

While inside the noisy machine, Vera was administered another quiz.

What type of bread are you?

Many of the quizzes centered around the importance of food. A scarcity society, poor things. She answered the questions as best she could, tapping on the ceiling-mounted console.

```
Toast. You are dead already and don't even know it yet.
```

This quiz result was unusually ominous, almost like a threat. Was the computer trying to warn her about something? Or maybe it was just trying to be helpful. Maybe Vera was dead and this was the afterlife. If this was the afterlife, it was not heaven because heaven should be perfectly understandable.

Death.

Vera remembered about death. The truth about death was like a password. Death was not for her and she was not located in her body. The real Vera was the version of her stored on the cloud. She was missing from her time and place, but she would be remade, redownloaded. She had probably already been replaced. Her boyfriend, if she had one, wouldn't know the difference. Her mother, if she had one, would be so relieved to have her back.

She was no longer Vera, she was a redundant Vera fragment. That was the password. The computer seemed to understand this.

What type of suicide are you?
```
Quick and painless. Scalpel to the carotid artery.
```

What do you get when you cut a worm in half?

This one wasn't a quiz. There were no questions to answer, just a big old button that said "enter" which Vera pressed.

```
Two worms.
```

Vera was rolled out of the large, noisy box and she stood up. She looked around the room. White countertop, white cabinets. There was a knife in here somewhere. The doctor was saying something to her, Vera ignored her. It was of no consequence. The instructions were clear. There could be only one true Vera and she was not it. The time machine was not the only way out.

There was banging outside. Shouting and gunshots? Or more monkeys with wrenches? The doctor looked alarmed and Vera felt fear for the first time since deciding to kill herself. The door burst open and women with armor and guns ran in. They all took their visors off at once. They all had the same face as Vera.

"We are here to rescue you," said one. Vera put her hands up in surrender and was escorted out the laboratory. Her first time outside since being born.

It felt strange to be marching among replicas. At least, it felt strange to Vera, but she saved her questions until they got into the limo.

"We are clones, right?" she asked, once safely ensconced in leather upholstery and dark glass.

A lookalike looked back at her. "We are not clones, we are incomplete downloads. You are incomplete download number 201. The real Vera is dead. Her backup file was corrupted. We are all that is left."

A different lookalike said: "You were kidnapped by past-worshipping hackers. They were trying to get the password for our Bejeweled account. We had forgotten about it until the breach was attempted. It's closed now."

Vera tapped her temples. The translation chip must be misfiring again, she couldn't understand most of what her others were trying to tell her.

"Then it's not the year 2014?" asked Vera. Several lookalikes laughed. One said: "OM24" as if that was supposed to clarify things. "Time travel is impossible," said another as if she didn't already know that.

"You should thank your beacon chip for helping us find you."

Vera tapped her temples again. Thank you, Brain. She tried to mean it even though she knew there was something wrong with Brain.

Vera's new house was a mansion she would be sharing with the 200 other downloads.

"You have to change your name. We can't all be Vera. I'm Wanda. I am the leader because I am the least damaged and the most like our original."

Vera tried to think of another name for herself, but she drew a blank.

"It's okay. You don't have to come up with your new name right now. It will probably be more difficult for you. No offense, but we think you are the most incomplete download. No offense, but we think you are probably retarded thanks to how sloppily you were downloaded."

Vera was silent for a minute. She wanted to say something smart to prove she was smart, but she could think of no response at all.

The other downloads had already been in existence for months since the breach of the original Vera origin file. Vera had only been in existence for a week because it had taken her months to be downloaded by her kidnappers. Despite the long manufacture time, they had done a botched job, so Vera #201, as she now thought of herself, had none of original Vera's memories or talents or personality.

In fact, Vera #201 thought her most striking feature was her lack of personality. Vera #201 had no talents, quirks or temper. She knew no jokes or magic tricks. This was in contrast to her 200 roommates, all incomplete, yet working to graft personalities onto the source code. Some could figure skate or do karate. Some were good at knitting or math. No two had very much in common, as if they were trying to occupy different, non-competitive niches. There was something very evolutionary and efficient about all of it. #201 was impressed by all of them. None of them were impressed by her.

"When I was in captivity, I filled out these questionnaires. They were supposed to tell me who I was. They were helpful in retrospect, I think."

"Are you referring to personality quizzes? They are stupid, everyone knows that," said Wanda.

"Well, I am also stupid, so I think they might help."

Wanda nodded in agreement. She loaded a quiz app onto a tablet and handed it to Vera #201.

"Good luck," she said.

What type of dinosaur are you?
Brontosaurus. You don't actually exist.

What type of toast are you?
Cinnamon toast. You were made by Mother.

What type of bizarre elephant relative are you?
The Gomotophere. You were also driven extinct by natives with spears.

Vera sighed and looked around the crowded rec room, filled to capacity with Vera-likes. The quizzes were making her feel more lonely. She needed a friend, someone nicer than Wanda. In the corner, she spotted Swamini Verananda deep in meditation. Her eyes were closed, her legs were tucked into lotus position and her entire body levitated two inches off the ground.

"Excuse me, Swamini? Would you mind taking a personality quiz?"

The Swamini opened her eyes. She practiced a religion of her own devising, but she never tried to convert anyone. She was the calmest Vera, she didn't even seem to mind being disturbed from her deep meditative state.

"What is the purpose of a personality quiz?" asked the Swamini.

"It is to discover the nature of the true self."

"What is the purpose of discovering the nature of the true self?"

"Because I am curious. I have been alive for nine days now and I keep waiting for someone to tell me who I am."

"Why are you waiting for someone else to tell you who you are?"

It was at this moment that Vera realized the Swamini only talked in questions. It was going to be hard to get her to answer a multiple choice personality quiz. In order to accommodate her new friend, Vera reconfigured the app so that it would accept the Swamini's questions as answers. But then the quiz results also came back as answers.

Q: What type of sailboat are you?
A: What type of sailboat should I be?

Q: What city should you live in
A: How can I feel connected to those around me no matter where I am?

Q: What type of data are you?
A: Why do we accept approximations of reality as a substitute for reality itself?

Vera #201 was unsatisfied by these results despite knowing they were meant to unsatisfy. The Swamini was trying to teach her about the illusion of certainty, or something. But a woman needed axioms. She needed theorems and corollaries. She needed to know what city she was born in, what vegetable she most resembled, what constellation best described her.

So Vera #201 went back to Wanda. Smug as she was, Wanda knew some things for sure. Wanda agreed to answer Vera's quizzes, because Wanda was very into helping the less fortunate.

Wanda was the kind of sailboat that could circumvent the globe. Wanda was New York because she was teeming with life. Wanda was big data because she was deep and contained many answers if you knew what questions to ask.

Wanda was in the middle of giving Vera a very inspiring pep talk when there was a knock at the mansion's front door. The door opened even before the butler could answer it.

It was a brand new lookalike, and #201 breathed a sigh of relief. She wasn't going to be the new kid anymore. But then the lookalike spoke, in a voice so clear and certain that Vera #201 knew what she was going to say before she said it.

"I am Vera 0.0. I am your original. I am not dead. There has been some kind of misunderstanding."

Wanda was mean in some ways, but also generous. She had assumed leadership of the Veras since she was the first and most complete download. She had converted the mansion into quarters for all of them. She had rescued each of the other Veras, even if it meant splitting the allowance an additional way. She had rescued #201, even though she was misshapen and asymmetric. Her face was sort of lumpy in places and one side of her body was puffier than the other.

Vera 0.0 didn't want to share her allowance, so she passed out personality quizzes. And after the results of the personality quizzes came in, she passed out eviction notices. Only #201 remained.

What is your mental age?

#201 got thirteen years old, which was way off considering she had only been alive for two weeks.

"What is your mental age?" she asked 0.0.

"Same as my physical age, thirty-one."

"What will happen to the others?"

"They will be fine. They will collect their pensions out of the victim's fund. They will find their own way in the world, separate from us. It's not good to live among your clones. It usually ends in resentment or murder."

There was an awkward silence.

"Anyway, it's better for them to scatter. Find themselves instead of trying to be me."

That's what they were doing already, #201 wanted to say.

"Why did you keep me? I am the worst one," asked #201.

"Is that what Wanda said? She was the worst one, I think. You are not the worst. You are thirteen. You are a brontosaurs. You are cinnamon toast. You are an expert in quizzes."

#201 nodded, because this was true. And, as so often happens, the quiz taker became the quiz master.

What day of the week are you?
What letter of the alphabet are you?
What ancient cave painting are you?

43

0.0 was Monday, she was the letter T, she was the multi-horned rhinoceros in Chauvet. She was calmer now that she had a reliable way of knowing who she was. So making questionnaires became #201's job. 0.0 preferred to interpret the results for herself, she did not like for #201 to tell her why she was Monday, or the letter T or the rhinoceros.

"What happened to you when you disappeared and everyone thought you were dead?" 0.0 had been kidnapped by a different cult of hackers, but she didn't want to talk about it or how she escaped. All she said was: "I was Thursday, I was the letter O, I was one of the cave paintings lost to time."

Quiz making for 0.0 didn't take up too much of #201's time, and #201 also didn't want to spend every moment with her original, especially not after the murder comment, so #201 took her quizzes to the street.

She would sit down, cross-legged like the Swamini, with a top hat for accepting donations in exchange for quizzes.

She would tell people what type of cold fusion they were or what type of personal transport they were and in exchange they would leave some thing in the hat, a button or a card. #201 didn't accept money, she wanted physical things. One time, someone left a pearl.

What type of pearl are you?

#201 was a baroque pearl, beautiful despite being misshapen. The other downloads found her, and eventually her main clientele was her cohort of others. Most of them lived together in an abandoned orphanage which they had remodeled. One hundred ninety seven of them all in one orphanage, the rest were finding themselves in Nepal. So far, no murder. They told #201 she could live there too, and maybe she would one day, if things with 0.0 got too weird.

They liked the quizzes because the quizzes made them feel like individuals. Otherwise there was a tendency to feel like a small lump of clay broken off from a larger and better one.

They wanted to know what kind of footwear they were, and it was up to #201 to tell them. It was up to #201 to say:

You are fuzzy slippers because you warm the soul.

You are running shoes because you will go very fast and very far.

You are stilettos and though you could kill someone, you probably won't.

You are shoes with a compartment for every toe. Everything fits.

ABOUT THE AUTHOR

Dominica Phetteplace is a graduate of the Clarion West Writer's Workshop and holds a degree in Mathematics from UC Berkeley. Her work has appeared in *Asimov's Science Fiction, PANK, The Los Angeles Review,* and *Flytrap.* She's currently a math tutor in Berkeley, California.

The Emperor of Mars
ALLEN M. STEELE

Out here, there's a lot of ways to go crazy. Get cooped up in a passenger module not much larger than a trailer, and by the time you reach your destination you may have come to believe that the universe exists only within your own mind: it's called solipsism syndrome, and I've seen it happen a couple of times. Share that same module with five or six guys who don't get along very well, and after three months you'll be sleeping with a knife taped to your thigh. Pull double-shifts during that time, with little chance to relax, and you'll probably suffer from depression; couple this with vitamin deficiency due to a lousy diet, and you're a candidate for chronic fatigue syndrome.

Folks who've never left Earth often think that Titan Plague is the main reason people go mad in space. They're wrong. Titan Plague may rot your brain and turn you into a homicidal maniac, but instances of it are rare, and there's a dozen other ways to go bonzo that are much more subtle. I've seen guys adopt imaginary friends with whom they have long and meaningless conversations, compulsively clean their hardsuits regardless of whether or not they've recently worn them, or go for a routine spacewalk and have to be begged to come back into the airlock. Some people just aren't cut out for life away from Earth, but there's no way to predict who's going to going to lose their mind.

When something like that happens, I have a set of standard procedures: ask the doctor to prescribe antidepressants, keep an eye on them to make sure they don't do anything that might put themselves or others at risk, relieve them of duty if I can, and see what I can do about getting them back home as soon as possible. Sometimes I don't have to do any of this. A guy goes crazy for a little while, and then he gradually works out whatever it was that got in his head; the next time I see him, he's in the commissary, eating Cheerios like nothing ever happened. Most of the time, though, a mental breakdown is a serious matter. I think I've shipped back about one out of every twenty people because of one issue or another.

But one time, I saw someone go mad, and it was the best thing that could have happened to him. That was Jeff Halbert. Let me tell about him . . .

Back in '48, I was General Manager of Arsia Station, the first and largest of the Mars colonies. This was a year before the formation of the Pax Astra, about five years before the colonies declared independence. So the six major Martian settlements were still under control of one Earth-based corporation or another, with Arsia Station owned and operated by ConSpace. We had about a hundred people living there by then, the majority short-timers on short-term contracts; only a dozen or so, like myself, were permanent residents who left Earth for good.

Jeff wasn't one of them. Like most people, he'd come to Mars to make a lot of money in a relatively short amount of time. Six months from Earth to Mars aboard a cycleship, two years on the planet, then six more months back to Earth aboard the next ship to make the crossing during the bi-annual launch window. In three years, a young buck like him could earn enough dough to buy a house, start a business, invest in the stock market, or maybe just loaf for a good long while. In previous times, they would've worked on off-shore oil rigs, joined the merchant marine, or built powersats; by mid-century, this kind of high-risk, high-paying work was on Mars, and there was no shortage of guys willing and ready to do it.

Jeff Halbert was what we called a "Mars monkey." We had about a lot of people like him at Arsia Station, and they took care of the dirty jobs that the scientists, engineers, and other specialists could not or would not handle themselves. One day they might be operating a bulldozer or a crane at a habitat construction site. The next day, they'd be unloading freight from a cargo lander that had just touched down. The day after that, they'd be cleaning out the air vents or repairing a solar array or unplugging a toilet. It wasn't romantic or particularly interesting work, but it was the sort of stuff that needed to be done in order to keep the base going, and because of that, kids like Jeff were invaluable.

And Jeff was definitely a kid. In his early twenties, wiry and almost too tall to wear a hardsuit, he looked like he'd started shaving only last week. Before he dropped out of school to get a job with ConSpace, I don't think he'd travelled more than a few hundred miles from the small town in New Hampshire where he'd grown up. I didn't know him well, but I knew his type: restless, looking for adventure, hoping to score a small pile of loot so that he could do something else with the rest of his life besides hang out in a pool hall. He probably hadn't even thought much about Mars before he spotted a ConSpace recruitment ad on some web site; he had two years of college, though, and met all the fitness requirements, and that was enough to get him into the training program and, eventually, a berth aboard a cycleship.

Before Jeff left Earth, he filled out and signed all the usual company paperwork. Among them was Form 36-B: Family Emergency Notification Consent. ConSpace required everyone to state whether or not they wanted to informed of a major illness or death of a family member back home. This was something a lot of people didn't take into consideration before they went to Mars, but nonetheless it was an issue that had to be addressed. If you found out, for instance, that your father was about to die, there wasn't much you could do about it, because you'd be at least 35 million miles from home. The best you could do would be to send a brief message that someone might be able to read to him before he passed away; you wouldn't be able to attend the funeral, and it would be many months, even a year or two, before you could lay roses on his grave.

Most people signed Form 36-D on the grounds that they'd rather know about something like this than be kept in the dark until they returned home. Jeff did, too, but I'd later learn that he hadn't read it first. For him, it had been just one more piece of paper that needed to be signed before he boarded the shuttle, not to be taken any more seriously than the catastrophic accident disclaimer or the form attesting that he didn't have any sort of venereal disease.

He probably wished he hadn't signed that damn form. But he did, and it cost him his sanity.

Jeff had been on Mars for only about seven months when a message was relayed from ConSpace's human resources office. I knew about it because a copy was cc'd to me. The minute I read it, I dropped what I was doing to head straight for Hab 2's second level, which was where the monkey house—that is, the dormitory for unspecialized laborers like Jeff—was located. I didn't have to ask which bunk was his; the moment I walked in, I spotted a knot of people standing around a young guy slumped on this bunk, staring in disbelief at the fax in his hands.

Until then, I didn't know, nor did anyone one at Arsia Station, that Jeff had a fiancé back home, a nice girl named Karen whom he'd met in high school and who had agreed to marry him about the same time he'd sent his application to ConSpace. Once he got the job, they decided to postpone the wedding until he returned, even if it meant having to put their plans on hold for three years. One of the reasons why Jeff decided to get a job on Mars, in fact, was to provide a nest egg for him and Karen. And they'd need it, too; about three weeks before Jeff took off, Karen informed him that she was pregnant and that he'd have a child waiting for him when he got home.

He'd kept this a secret, mainly because he knew that the company would annul his contract if it learned that he had a baby on the way. Both Jeff's family and Karen's knew all about the baby, though, and they decided to pretend that Jeff was still on Earth, just away on a long business trip. Until he returned, they'd take care of Karen.

About three months before the baby was due, the two families decided to host a baby shower. The party was to be held at the home of one of Jeff's uncles—apparently he was only relative with a house big enough for such a get-together—and Karen was on her way there, in a car driven by Jeff's parents, when tragedy struck. Some habitual drunk who'd learned how to disable his car's high-alcohol lockout, and therefore was on the road when he shouldn't have been, plowed straight into them. The drunk walked away with no more than a sprained neck, but his victims were nowhere nearly so lucky. Karen, her unborn child, Jeff's mother and father—all died before they reached the hospital.

There's not a lot you can say to someone who's just lost his family that's going to mean very much. *I'm sorry* barely scratches the surface. *I understand what you're going through* is ridiculous; *I know how you feel* is insulting. And *is there anything I can do to help?* is pointless unless you have a time machine; if I did, I would have lent it to Jeff, so that he could travel back twenty-four hours to call his folks and beg them to put off picking up Karen by only fifteen or twenty minutes. But everyone said these things anyway, because there wasn't much else that *could* be said, and I relieved Jeff of further duties until he felt like he was ready to go to work again, because there was little else I could do for him. The next cycleship wasn't due to reach Mars for another seventeen months; by the time he got home, his parents and Karen would be dead for nearly two years.

To Jeff's credit, he was back on the job within a few days. Maybe he knew that there was nothing he could do except work, or maybe he just got tired of staring at the walls. In any case, one morning he put on his suit, cycled through the airlock, and went outside to help the rest of the monkeys dig a pit for the new septic tank. But he wasn't the same easy-going kid we'd known before; no wisecracks, no goofing off, not even any gripes about the hours it took to make that damn hole and how he'd better get overtime for this. He was like a robot out there, silently digging at the sandy red ground with a shovel, until the pit was finally finished, at which point he dropped his tools and, without a word, returned to the hab, where he climbed out of his suit and went to the mess hall for some chow.

A couple of weeks went by, and there was no change. Jeff said little to anyone. He ate, worked, slept, and that was about it. When you looked into his eyes, all you saw was a distant stare. If he'd broken down in hysterics, I would've understood, but there wasn't any of that. It was as if he'd shut down his emotions, suppressing whatever he was feeling inside.

The station had a pretty good hospital by then, large enough to serve all the colonies, and Arsia General's senior psychologist had begun meeting with Jeff on a regular basis. Three days after Jeff went back to work, Karl Rosenfeld dropped by my office. His report was grim: Jeff Halbert was suffering from severe depression, to the point that he was barely responding to medication. Although he hadn't spoken of suicide, Dr. Rosenfeld had little doubt that the notion had occurred to him. And I knew that, if Jeff did decide to kill himself, all he'd have to do was wait until the next time he went outside, then shut down his suit's air supply and crack open the helmet faceplate. One deep breath, and the Martian atmosphere would do the rest; he'd be dead before anyone could reach him.

"You want my advice?" Karl asked, sitting on the other side of my desk with a glass of moonshine in hand. "Find something that'll get his mind off what happened."

"You think that hasn't occurred to me? Believe me, I've tried . . . "

"Yeah, I know. He told me. But extra work shifts aren't helping, and neither are vids or games." He was quiet for a moment, "If I thought sex would help," he added, "I'd ask a girl I know to haul him off to bed, but that would just make matters worse. His fiancé was the only woman he ever loved, and it'll probably be a long time before he sleeps with anyone again."

"So what do you want me to do?" I gave a helpless shrug. "C'mon, give me a clue here. I want to help the kid, but I'm out of ideas."

"Well . . . I looked at the duty roster, and saw that you've scheduled a survey mission for next week. Something up north, I believe."

"Uh-huh. I'm sending a team up there to see if they can locate a new water supply. Oh, and one of the engineers wants to make a side-trip to look at an old NASA probe."

"So put Jeff on the mission." Karl smiled. "They're going to need a monkey or two anyway. Maybe travel will do him some good."

His suggestion was as good as any, so I pulled up the survey assignment list, deleted the name of one monkey, and inserted Jeff Halbert's instead. I figured it couldn't hurt, and I was right. And also wrong.

So Jeff was put on a two-week sortie that travelled above the 60th parallel to the Vastitas Borealis, the subarctic region that surrounds the Martian north pole. The purpose of the mission was to locate a site for a new well. Although most of Arsia Station's water came from atmospheric condensers and our greenhouses, we needed more than they could supply, which was why we drilled artesian wells in the permafrost beneath the northern tundra and pump groundwater to surface tanks, which in turn would be picked up on a monthly basis. Every few years or so, one of those wells would run dry; when that happened, we'd have to send a team up there to dig a new one.

Two airships made the trip, the *Sagan* and the *Collins.* Jeff Halbert was aboard the *Collins,* and according to its captain, who was also the mission leader, he did his job well. Over the course of ten days, the two dirigibles roamed the tundra, stopping every ten or fifteen miles so that crews could get out and conduct test drills that would bring up a sample of what lay beneath the rocky red soil. It wasn't hard work, really, and it gave Jeff a chance to see the northern regions. Yet he was quiet most of the time, rarely saying much to anyone; in fact, he seemed to be bored by the whole thing. The other people on the expedition were aware of what had recently happened to him, of course, and they attempted to draw him out of his shell, but after awhile it became obvious that he just didn't want to talk, and so they finally gave up and left him alone.

Then, on the eleventh day of the mission, two days before the expedition was scheduled to return to Arsia, the *Collins* located the Phoenix lander.

This was a NASA probe that landed back in `08, the first to confirm the presence of subsurface ice on Mars. Unlike many of the other American and European probes that explored Mars before the first manned expeditions, Phoenix didn't have a rover; instead, it used a robotic arm to dig down into the regolith, scooping up samples that were analyzed by its onboard chemical lab. The probe was active for only a few months before its battery died during the long Martian winter, but it was one of the milestones leading to human colonization.

As they expected, the expedition members found Phoenix half-buried beneath wind-blown sand and dust, with only its upper platform and solar vanes still exposed. Nonetheless, the lander was intact, and although it was too big heavy to be loaded aboard the airship, the crew removed its arm to be taken home and added to the base museum. And they found one more thing: the Mars library.

During the 1990's, while the various Mars missions were still in their planning stages, the Planetary Society had made a proposal to NASA: one of those probes should carry a DVD containing a cache of literature, visual images, and audio recordings pertaining to Mars. The ostensive purpose would be to furnish future colonists with a library for their entertainment, but the unspoken reason was to pay tribute to the generations of writers, artists, and filmmakers whose works had inspired the real-life exploration of Mars.

NASA went along with those proposal, so a custom-designed DVD, made of silica glass to ensure its long-term survival, was prepared for inclusion on a future mission. A panel selected 84 novels, short stories, articles, and speeches, with the authors ranging from 18th century fantasists like Swift and Voltaire to 20th century science fiction authors like Niven and Benford. A digital gallery of 60 visual images—including everything from paintings by Bonestell, Emshwiller, and Whelan to a lobby card from a Flash Gordon serial and a cover of a *Weird Science* comic book—was chosen as well. The final touch were four audio clips, the most notable of which were the infamous 1938 radio broadcast of *The War of the Worlds* and a discussion of the same between H.G. Wells and Orson Welles.

Now called "Visions of Mars," the disk was originally placed aboard NASA's Mars Polar Lander, but that probe was destroyed when its booster failed shortly after launch and it crashed in the Atlantic. So an identical copy was put on Phoenix, and this time it succeeded in getting to Mars. And so the disk had remained in the Vastitas Borealis for the past forty years, awaiting the day when a human hand would remove it from its place on Phoenix's upper fuselage.

And that hand happened to be Jeff Halbert's.

The funny thing is, no one on the expedition knew the disk was there. It had been forgotten by then, its existence buried deep within the old NASA documents I'd been sent from Earth, so I hadn't told anyone to retrieve it. And besides, most of the guys on the *Collins* were more interested in taking a look at an antique lander than the DVD that happened to be attached to it. So when Jeff found the disk and detached it from Phoenix, it wasn't like he'd made a major find. The attitude of almost everyone on the mission was *oh, yeah, that's kind of neat . . . take it home and see what's on it.*

Which was easier said than done. DVD drives had been obsolete for more than twenty years, and the nearest flea market where one might find an old computer that had one was . . . well, it wasn't on Mars. But Jeff looked around, and eventually he found a couple of dead comps stashed in a storage closet, salvage left over from the first expeditions. Neither were usable on their own, but with the aid of a service manual, he was able to swap out enough parts to get one of them up and running, and once it was operational, he removed the disk from its scratched case and gently slid it into the slot. Once he was sure that the data was intact and hadn't decayed, he downloaded everything into his personal pad. And then, at random, he selected one of the items on the menu—"The Martian Way" by Isaac Asimov—and began to read.

Why did Jeff go to so much trouble? Perhaps he wanted something to do with his free time besides mourn for the dead. Or maybe he wanted to show the others who'd been on the expedition that they shouldn't have ignored the disk. I don't know for sure, so I can't tell you. All I know is that the disk first interested him, then intrigued him, and finally obsessed him.

It took awhile for me to become aware of the change in Jeff. As much as I was concerned for him, he was one of my lesser problems. As general manager, on any given day I had a dozen or more different matters that needed my attention, whether it be making sure that the air recycling system was repaired before we suffocated to death or filling out another stack of forms sent from Huntsville. So Jeff wasn't always on my mind; when I didn't hear from Dr. Rosenfeld for awhile, I figured that the two of them had managed to work out his issues, and turned to other things.

Still, there were warning signs, stuff that I noticed but to which I didn't pay much attention. Like the day I was monitoring the radio crosstalk from the monkeys laying sewage pipes in the foundation of Hab Three, and happened to hear Jeff identify himself as Lieutenant Gulliver Jones. The monkeys sometimes screwed around like that on the com channels, and the foreman told Halbert to knock it off and use his proper call sign . . . but when Jeff answered him, his response was weird: *"Aye, sir. I was simply ruminating on the rather peculiar environment in which we've found ourselves."* He even faked a British accent to match the Victorian diction. That got a laugh from the other monkeys, but nonetheless I wondered who Gulliver Jones was and why Jeff was pretending to be him.

There was also the time Jeff was out on a dozer, clearing away the sand that had been deposited on the landing field during a dust storm a couple of days earlier. Another routine job to which I hadn't been paying much attention until the shift supervisor at the command center paged me: *"Chief, there's something going on with Halbert. You might want to listen in."*

So I tapped into the comlink, and there was Jeff: *"Affirmative, MainCom. I just saw something move out there, about a half-klick north of the periphery."*

"Roger that, Tiger Four-Oh," the supervisor said. *"Can you describe again, please?"*

A pause, then: *"A big creature, abut ten feet tall, with eight legs. And there was a woman riding it . . . red-skinned, and–"* an abrupt laugh *"— stark naked, or just about."*

Something tugged at my memory, but I couldn't quite put my finger on it. When the shift supervisor spoke again, his voice had a patronizing undertone. *"Yeah . . . uh, right, Tiger Four-Oh. We just checked the LRC, though, and there's nothing on the scope except you."*

"They're gone now. Went behind a boulder and vanished." Another laugh, almost gleeful. *"But they were out there, I promise!"*

"Affirmative, Four-Oh." A brief pause. *"If you happen to see any more thoats, let us know, okay?"*

That's when I remembered. What Jeff had described was a beast from Edgar Rice Burroughs' Mars novels. And the woman riding it? That could have only been Dejah Thoris. Almost everyone who came to Mars read Burroughs at one point or another, but this was the first time I'd ever heard of anyone claiming to have seen the Princess of Helium.

Obviously, Jeff had taken to playing practical jokes. I made a mental note to say something to him about that, but then forgot about it. As I said, on any given day I handled any number of different crises, and someone messing with his supervisor's head ranked low on my priority list.

But that wasn't the end of it. In fact, it was only the beginning. A couple of weeks later, I received a memo from the quartermaster: someone had tendered a request to be transferred to private quarters, even though that was above his pay-grade. At Arsia in those days, before we got all the habs built, individual rooms were at a premium and were generally reserved for management, senior researchers, married couples, company stooges, and so forth. In this case, though, the other guys in this particular person's dorm had signed a petition backing his request, and the quartermaster himself wrote that, for the sake of morale, he was recommending that this individual be assigned his own room.

I wasn't surprised to see that Jeff Halbert was the person making the request. By then, I'd noticed that his personality had undergone a distinct change. He'd let his hair grow long, eschewing the high-and-tight style preferred by people who spent a lot of time wearing a hardsuit helmet. He rarely shared a table with anyone else in the wardroom, and instead ate by himself, staring at his datapad the entire time. And he was now talking to himself on the comlink. No more reports of Martian princesses riding eight-legged animals, but rather a snatch of this ("The Martians seem to have calculated their descent with amazing subtlety . . . ") or a bit of that ("The Martians gazed back up at them for a long, long silent time from the rippling water . . . ") which most people wouldn't have recognized as being quotes from Wells or Bradbury.

So it was no wonder the other monkey house residents wanted to get rid of him. Before I signed the request, though, I paid Dr. Rosenfeld a visit. The station psychologist didn't have to ask why I was there; he asked me to shut the door, then let me know what he thought about Jeff.

"To tell the truth," he began, "I can't tell if he's getting better or worse."

"I can. Look, I'm no shrink, but if you ask me, he's getting worse."

Karl shook his head. "Not necessarily. Sure, his behavior is bizarre, but at least we no longer have to worry about suicide. In fact, he's one of the happiest people we have here. He rarely speaks about his loss anymore, and when I remind him that his wife and parents are dead, he shrugs it off as if this was something that happened a long time ago. In his own way, he's quite content with life."

"And you don't think that's strange?"

"Sure, I do . . . especially since he's admitted to me that he'd stopped taking the anti-depressants I prescribed to him. And that's the bad news. Perhaps he isn't depressed anymore, or at least by clinical standards . . . but he's becoming delusional, to the point of actually having hallucinations."

I stared at him. "You mean, the time he claimed he spotted Dejah Thoris . . . you're saying he actually *saw* that?"

"Yes, I believe so. And that gave me a clue as to what's going on in his mind." Karl picked up a penknife, absently played with it. "Ever since he found that disk, he's become utterly obsessed with it. So I asked him if he'd let me copy it from his pad, which he did, and after I asked him what he was reading, I checked it out for myself. And what I discovered was that, of all the novels and stories that are on the disk, the ones that attract him the most are also the ones that are least representative of reality. That is, the stuff that's about Mars, but not as we know it."

"Come again?" I shook my head. "I don't understand."

"How much science fiction have you read?"

"A little. Not much."

"Well, lucky for you, I've read quite a bit." He grinned. "In fact, you could say that's why I'm here. I got hooked on that stuff when I was a kid, and by the time I got out of college, I'd pretty much decided that I wanted to see Mars." He became serious again. "Okay, try to follow me. Although people have been writing about Mars since the 1700's, it wasn't until the first Russian and American probes got out here in the 1960's that anyone knew what this place is really like. That absence of knowledge gave writers and artists the liberty to fill in the gap with their imaginations... or at least until they learned better. Understand?"

"Sure." I shrugged. "Before the 1960's, you could have Martians. After that, you couldn't have Martians anymore."

"Umm... well, not exactly." Karl lifted his hand, teetered it back and forth. "One of the best stories on the disk is 'A Rose For Ecclesiastes' by Roger Zelazny. It was written in 1963, and it has Martians in it. And some stories written before then were pretty close to getting it right. But for the most part, yes... the fictional view of Mars changed dramatically in the second half of the last century, and although it became more realistic, it also lost much of its romanticism."

Karl folded the penknife, dropped it on his desk. "Those aren't the stories Jeff's reading. Greg Bear's 'A Martian Ricorso,' Arthur C. Clarke's 'Transit of Earth,' John Varley's 'In the Hall of the Martian Kings'... anything similar to the Mars we know, he ignores. Why? Because they remind him of where he is... and that's not where he wants to be."

"So ... " I thought about it for a moment. "He's reading the older stuff instead?"

"Right." Karl nodded. "Stanley Weinbaum's 'A Martian Odyssey,' Otis Albert Kline's 'The Swordsman of Mars,' A.E. van Vogt's 'The Enchanted Village'... the more unreal, the more he likes them. Because those stories aren't about not the drab, lifeless planet where he's stuck, but instead a planet of native Martians, lost cities, canal systems ... "

"Okay, I get it."

"No, I don't think you do... because I'm not sure I do, either, except to say that Jeff appears to be leaving us. Every day, he's taking one more step into this other world... and I don't think he's coming back again."

I stared at him, not quite believing what I'd just heard. "Jeez, Karl... what am I going to do?"

"What *can* you do?" He leaned back in his chair. "Not much, really. Look, I'll be straight with you... this is beyond me. He needs the kind of treatment that I can't give him here. For that, he's going to have to wait until he gets back to Earth."

"The next ship isn't due for another fourteen months or so."

"I know... that's when I'm scheduled to go back, too. But the good news is that he's happy and reasonably content, and doesn't really pose a threat to anyone . . . except maybe by accident, in which case I'd recommend that you relieve him of any duties that would take him outside the hab."

"Done." The last thing anyone needed was to have a delusional person out on the surface. Mars can be pretty unforgiving when it comes to human error, and a fatal mistake can cost you not only your own life, but also the guy next to you. "And I take it that you recommend that his request be granted, too?"

"It wouldn't hurt, no." A wry smile. "So long as he's off in his own world, he'll be happy. Make him comfortable, give him whatever he wants . . . within reason, at least . . . and leave him alone. I'll keep an eye on him and will let you know if his condition changes, for better or worse."

"Hopefully for the better."

"Sure . . . but I wouldn't count on it." Karl stared straight at me. "Face it, chief . . . one of your guys is turning into a Martian."

I took Jeff off the outside-work details and let it be known that he wasn't permitted to go marswalking without authorization or an escort, and instead reassigned him to jobs that would keep him in the habitats: working in the greenhouse, finishing the interior of Hab 2, that sort of thing. I was prepared to tell him that he was being taken off the outside details because he'd reached his rem limit for radiation exposure, but he never questioned my decision but only accepted it with the same quiet, spooky smile that he'd come to giving everyone.

I also let him relocate to private quarters, a small room on Hab 2's second level that had been unoccupied until then. As I expected, there were a few gripes from those still having to share a room with someone else; however, most people realized that Jeff was in bad shape and needed his privacy. After he moved in, though, he did something I didn't anticipate: he changed his door lock's password to something no one else knew. This was against station rules—the security office and the general manager were supposed to always have everyone's lock codes—but Karl assured me that Jeff meant no harm. He simply didn't want to have anyone enter his quarters, and it would help his peace of mind if he received this one small exemption. I went along with it, albeit reluctantly.

After that, I had no problems with Jeff for awhile. He assumed his new duties without complaint, and the reports I received from department heads told me that he was doing his work well. Karl updated me every week; his patient hadn't yet shown any indications of snapping out of his fugue, but neither did he appear to be getting worse. And although he was no longer interacting with any other personnel except when he needed to, at least he was no longer telling anyone about Martian princesses or randomly quoting obscure science fiction stories over the comlink.

Nonetheless, there was the occasional incident. Such as when the supply chief came to me with an unusual request Jeff had made: several reams of hemp paper, and as much soy ink as could be spared. Since both were by-products of greenhouse crops grown at either Arsia Station or one of the other colonies, and thus not imported from Earth, they weren't particularly scarce. Still, what could Jeff possibly want with that much writing material? I asked Karl if Jeff had told him that he was keeping a journal; the doctor told me that he hadn't, but unless either paper or ink were in short supply, it couldn't hurt to grant that request. So I signed off on this as well, although I told the supply chief to subtract the cost from Jeff's salary.

Not long after that, I heard from one of the communications officers. Jeff had asked her to send a general memo to the other colonies: a request for downloads of any Mars novels or stories that their personnel might have. The works of Bradbury, Burroughs, and Brackett were particularly desired, although stuff by Moorcock, Williamson, and Sturgeon would also be appreciated. In exchange, Jeff would send stories and novels he'd downloaded from the Phoenix disk.

Nothing wrong there, either. By then, Mars was on the opposite side of the Sun from Earth, so Jeff couldn't make the same request from Huntsville. If he was running out of reading material, then it made sense that he'd have to go begging from the other colonies. In fact, the com officer told me she'd had already received more than a half-dozen downloads; apparently quite a few folks had Mars fiction stashed in the comps. Nonetheless, it was unusual enough that she thought I should know about it. I asked her to keep me posted, and shrugged it off as just another of a long series of eccentricities.

A few weeks after that, though, Jeff finally did something that rubbed me the wrong way. As usual, I heard about it Dr. Rosenfeld.

"Jeff has a new request," he said when I happened to drop by his office. "In the future, he would prefer to be addressed as 'Your Majesty' or 'Your Highness,' in keeping with his position as the Emperor of Mars."

I stared at him for several seconds. "Surely you're joking," I said at last.

"Surely I'm not. He is now the Emperor Jeffery the First, sovereign monarch of the Great Martian Empire, warlord and protector of the red planet." A pause, during which I expected Karl to grin and wink. He didn't. "He doesn't necessarily want anyone bow in his presence," he added, "but he does require proper respect for the crown."

"I see." I closed my eyes, rubbed the bridge of my nose between my thumb and forefinger, and counted to ten. "And what does that make me?"

"Prime Minister, of course." The driest of smiles. "Since his title is hereditary, His Majesty isn't interested in the day-to-day affairs of his empire. That he leaves up to you, with the promise that he'll refrain from meddling with your decisions . . . "

"Oh, how fortunate I am."

"Yes. But from here on, all matters pertaining to the throne should be taken up with me, in my position as Royal Physician and Senior Court Advisor."

"Uh-huh." I stood up from my chair. "Well, if you'll excuse me, I think the Prime Minister needs to go now and kick His Majesty's ass."

"Sit down." Karl glared at me. "Really, I mean it. Sit."

I was unwilling to sit down again, but neither did I storm out of his office. "Look, I know he's a sick man, but this has gone far enough. I've given him his own room, relieved him of hard labor, given him paper and ink . . . for what, I still don't know, but he keeps asking for more . . . and allowed him com access to the other colonies. Just because he's been treated like a king doesn't mean he *is* a king."

"Oh, I agree. Which is why I've reminded him that his title is honorary as well as hereditary, and as such there's a limit to royal privilege. And he understands this. After all, the empire is in decline, having reached its peak over a thousand years ago, and since then the emperor has had to accept certain sacrifices for the good of the people. So, no, you won't see him wearing a crown and carrying a scepter, nor will he be demanding that a throne be built for him. He wants his reign to be benign."

Hearing this, I reluctantly took my seat again. "All right, so let me get this straight. He believes that he's now a king . . . "

"An emperor. There's a difference."

"King, emperor, whatever . . . he's not going to be bossing anyone around, but will pretty much let things continue as they are. Right?"

"Except that he wants to be addressed formally, yeah, that's pretty much it." Karl sighed, shook his head. "Let me try to explain. Jeff has come face-to-face with a reality that he cannot bear. His parents, his fiancé, the child they wanted to have . . . they're all dead, and he was too far away to prevent it, or even go to their funerals. This is a very harsh reality that he needs to keep at bay, so he's built a wall around himself . . . a wall of delusion, if you will. At first, it took the form of an obsession with fantasy, but when that wouldn't alone suffice, he decided to enter that fantasy, become part of it. This is where Emperor Jeffery the First of the Great Martian Empire comes in."

"So he's protecting himself?"

"Yes . . . by creating a role that lets him believe that he controls his own life." Karl shook his head. "He doesn't want to actually run Arsia, chief. He just wants to pretend that he does. As long as you allow him this, he'll be all right. Trust me."

"Well . . . all right." Not that I had much choice in the matter. If I was going to have a crazy person in my colony, at least I could make sure that he wouldn't endanger anyone. If that meant indulging him until he could be sent back to Earth, then that was what I'd have to do. "I'll pass the word that His Majesty is to be treated with all due respect."

"That would be great. Thanks." Karl smiled. "Y'know, people have been pretty supportive. I haven't heard of anyone taunting him."

"You know how it is. People here tend to look out for each other . . . they have to." I stood up and started to head for the door, then another thought occurred to me. "Just one thing. Has he ever told you what he's doing in his room? Like I said, he's been using a lot of paper and ink."

"Yes, I've noticed the ink stains on his fingers." Karl shook his head. "No, I don't. I've asked him about that, and the only thing he's told me is that he's preparing a gift for his people, and that he'll allow us to see it when the time comes."

"A gift?" I raised an eyebrow. "Any idea what it is?"

"Not a clue . . . but I'm sure we'll find out."

I kept my promise to Dr. Rosenfeld and put out the word that Jeff Halbert was heretofore to be known as His Majesty, the Emperor. As I told Karl, people were generally accepting of this. Oh, I heard the occasional report of someone giving Jeff some crap about this—exaggerated bows in the corridors, ill-considered questions about who was going to be his queen, and so forth—but the jokers who did this were usually pulled aside and told to shut up. Everyone at Arsia knew that Jeff was mentally ill, and that the best anyone could do for him was to let him have his fantasy life for as long as he was with us.

By then, Earth was no longer on the other side of the Sun. Once our home world and Mars began moving toward conjunction, a cycleship could the trip home. So only a few months remained until Jeff would board a shuttle. Since Karl would be returning as well, I figured he'd be in good hands, or at least they climbed into zombie tanks to hibernate for the long ride to Earth. Until then, all we had to do was keep His Majesty happy.

That wasn't hard to do. In fact, Karl and I had a lot of help. Once people got used to the idea that a make-believe emperor lived among them, most of them actually seemed to enjoy the pretense. When he walked through the habs, folks would pause whatever they were doing to nod to him and say "Your Majesty" or "Your Highness." He was always allowed to go to the front of the serving line in the mess hall, and there was always someone ready to hold his chair for him. And I noticed that he even picked up a couple of consorts, two unattached young women who did everything from trim his hair—it had grown very long by then, with a regal beard to match—to assist him in the Royal Gardens (aka the greenhouse) to accompany him to the Saturday night flicks. As one of the girls told me, the Emperor was the perfect date: always the gentleman, he'd unfailingly treated them with respect and never tried to take advantage of them. Which was more than could be said for some of the single men at Arsia.

After awhile, I relaxed the rule about not letting him leave the habs, and allowed him to go outside as long as he was under escort at all times. Jeff remembered how to put on a hardsuit,—a sign that he hadn't completely lost touch with reality—and he never gave any indication that he was on the verge of opening his helmet. But once he walked a few dozen yards from the airlock, he'd often stop and stare into the distance for a very long time, keeping his back to the rest of the base and saying nothing to anyone.

I wondered what he was seeing then. Was it a dry red desert, cold and lifeless, with rocks and boulders strewn across an arid plain beneath a pink sky? Or did he see something no one else could: forests of giant lichen, ancient canals upon which sailing vessels slowly glided, cities as old as time from which John Carter and Tars Tarkas rode to their next adventure or where tyrants called for the head of the outlaw Eric John Stark. Or was he thinking of something else entirely? A mother and a father who'd raised him, a woman he'd once loved, a child whom he'd never see?

I don't know, for the Emperor seldom spoke to me, even in my role as his Prime Minister. I think I was someone he wanted to avoid, an authority figure who had the power to shatter his illusions. Indeed, in all the time that Jeff was with us, I don't think he and I said more than a few words to each other. In fact, it wasn't until the day that he finally left for Earth that he said anything of consequence to me.

That morning, I drove him and Dr. Rosenfeld out to the landing field, where a shuttle was waiting to transport them up to the cycleship. Jeff was unusually quiet; I couldn't easily see his expression through his helmet faceplate, but the few glimpses I had told me that he wasn't happy. His Majesty knew that he was leaving his empire. Karl hadn't softened the blow by telling him a convenient lie, but instead had given him the truth: they were returning to Earth, and he'd probably never see Mars again.

Their belongings had already been loaded aboard the shuttle when we arrived, and the handful of other passengers were waiting to climb aboard. I parked the rover at the edge of the landing field and escorted Jeff and Karl to the spacecraft. I shook hands with Karl and wished him well, then turned to Jeff.

"Your Majesty . . . " I began.

"You don't have to call me that," he said.

"Pardon me?"

Jeff stepped closer to me. "I know I'm not really an emperor. That was something I got over a while ago . . . I just didn't want to tell anyone."

I glanced at Karl. His eyes were wide, and within his helmet he shook his head. This was news to him, too. "Then . . . you know who you really are?"

A brief flicker of a smile. "I'm Jeff Halbert. There's something wrong with me, and I don't really know what it is . . . but I know that I'm Jeff Halbert and that I'm going home." He hesitated, then went on. "I know we haven't talked much, but I . . . well, Dr. Rosenfeld has told me what you've done for me, and I just wanted to thank you. For putting up with me all this time, and for letting me be the Emperor of Mars. I hope I haven't been too much trouble."

I slowly let out my breath. My first thought was that he'd been playing me and everyone else for fools, but then I realized that his megalomania had probably been real, at least for a time. In any case, it didn't matter now; he was on his way back to Earth, the first steps on the long road to recovery.

Indeed, many months later, I received a letter from Karl. Shortly after he returned to Earth, Jeff was admitted to a private clinic in southern Vermont, where he began a program of psychiatric treatment. The process had been painful; as Karl had deduced, Jeff's mind had repressed the knowledge of his family's deaths, papering over the memory with fantastical delusions he'd derived from the stories he'd been reading. The clinic psychologists agreed with Dr. Rosenfeld: it was probably the retreat into fantasy that saved Jeff's life, by providing him with a place to which he was able to escape when his mind was no longer able to cope with a tragic reality. And in the end, when he no longer needed that illusion, Jeff returned from madness. He'd never see a Martian princess again, or believe himself to be the ruling monarch of the red planet.

But that was yet to come. I bit my tongue and offered him my hand. "No trouble, Jeff. I just hope everything works out for you."

"Thanks." Jeff shook my hand, then turned away to follow Karl to the ladder. Then he stopped and looked back at me again. "One more thing . . . "

"Yes?"

"There's something in my room I think you'd like to see. I disabled the lock just before I left, so you won't need the password to get in there." A brief pause. "It was `Thuvia,' just in case you need it anyway."

"Thank you." I peered at him. "So . . . what's is it?"

"Call it a gift from the emperor," he said.

I walked back to the rover and waited until the shuttle lifted off, then I drove to Hab 2. When I reached Jeff's room, though, I discovered that I wasn't the first person to arrive. Several of his friends—his fellow monkeys, the emperor's consorts, a couple of others—had already opened the door and gone in. I heard their astonished murmurs as I walked down the hall, but it wasn't until I pushed entered the room that I saw what amazed them.

Jeff's quarters were small, but he'd done a lot with it over the last year and a half. The wall above his bed was covered with sheets of paper that he'd taped together, upon which he'd drawn an elaborate mural. Here was the Mars over which the Emperor had reigned: boat-like aircraft hovering above great domed cities, monstrous creatures prowling red wastelands, bare-chested heroes defending beautiful women with rapiers and radium pistols, all beneath twin moons that looked nothing like the Phobos and Deimos we knew. The mural was crude, yet it had been rendered with painstaking care, and was nothing like anything we'd ever seen before.

That wasn't all. On the desk next to the comp was the original Phoenix disk, yet Jeff hadn't been satisfied just to leave it behind. A wire-frame bookcase had been built beside the desk, and neatly stacked upon its shelves were dozens of sheaves of paper, some thick and some thin, each carefully bound with hemp twine. Books, handwritten and handmade.

I carefully pulled down one at random, gazed at its title page: *Edison's Conquest of Mars* by Garrett P. Serviss. I put it back on the shelf, picked up another: "Omnilingual" by H. Beam Piper. I placed it on the shelf, then pulled down yet another: *The Martian Crown Jewels,* by Poul Anderson. And more, dozens more . . .

This was what Jeff had been doing all this time: transcribing the contents of the Phoenix disk, word by word. Because he knew, in spite of his madness, that he couldn't stay on Mars forever, and he wanted to leave something behind. A library, so that others could enjoy the same stories that had helped him through a dark and troubled time.

The library is still here. In fact, we've improved it quite a bit. I had the bed and dresser removed, and replaced them with armchairs and reading lamps. The mural has been preserved within glass frames, and the books have been rebound inside plastic covers. The Phoenix disk is gone, but its contents have been downloaded into a couple of comps; the disk itself is in the base museum. And we've added a lot of books to the shelves; every time a cycleship arrives from Earth, it brings more a few more volumes for our collection. It's become one of the favorite places in Arsia for people to relax. There's almost always someone there, sitting in a chair with a novel or story in his or her lap.

The sign on the door reads *Imperial Martian Library*: an inside joke that newcomers and tourists don't get. And, yes, I've spent a lot of time there myself. It's never too late to catch up on the classics.

First published in *Asimov's Science Fiction,* June 2010.

ABOUT THE AUTHOR

Allen Steele made his first sale in 1988. In 1990, he published his critically-acclaimed first novel, *Orbital Decay,* which subsequently won the Locus Poll as Best First Novel of the year, and soon Steele was being compared to Golden Age Heinlein by no less an authority than Gregory Benford. His other books include the novels *Clarke County Space, Lunar Descent, Labyrinth of Night, The Weight, The Tranquility Alternative, A King of Infinite Space, Oceanspace, Chronospace, Coyote, Coyote Rising, Spindrift, Galaxy Blues, Coyote Horizon, Coyote Destiny, Hex,* and a YA novel, *Apollo's Outcast.* His short work has been gathered in four collections, *Rude Astronauts, Sex and Violence in Zero G, The Last Science Fiction Writer,* and *Sex and Violence in Zero-G: The Complete "Near Space" Stories: Expanded Edition.* His most recent book is a new novel, *V-S Day.* He has won three Hugo Awards, in 1996 for his novella "The Death of Captain Future," in 1998 for his novella "Where Angels Fear to Tread," and, most recently, in 2011 for his novelette "The Emperor of Mars." Born in Nashville, Tennessee, he has worked for a variety of newspapers and magazines, covering science and business assignments, and is now a full-time writer living in Whately, Massachusetts with his wife Linda.

The Sledge-Maker's Daughter

ALASTAIR REYNOLDS

She stopped in sight of Twenty Arch Bridge, laying down her bags to rest her hands from the weight of two hog's heads and forty pence worth of beeswax candles. While she paused, Kathrin adjusted the drawstring on her hat, tilting the brim to shade her forehead from the sun. Though the air was still cool, there was a fierce new quality to the light that brought out her freckles.

Kathrin moved to continue, but a tightness in her throat made her hesitate. She had been keeping the bridge from her thoughts until this moment, but now the fact of it could not be ignored. Unless she crossed it she would face the long trudge to New Bridge, a diversion that would keep her on the road until long after sunset.

"Sledge-maker's daughter!" called a rough voice from across the road.

Kathrin turned sharply at the sound. An aproned man stood in a doorway, smearing his hands dry. He had a monkey-like face, tanned a deep liverish red, with white sideboards and a gleaming pink tonsure.

"Brendan Lynch's daughter, isn't it?"

She nodded meekly, but bit her lip rather than answer.

"Thought so. Hardly one to forget a pretty face, me." The man beckoned her to the doorway of his shop. "Come here, lass. I've something for your father."

"Sir?"

"I was hoping to visit him last week, but work kept me here." He cocked his head at the painted wooden trademark hanging above the doorway. "Peter Rigby, the wheelwright. Kathrin, isn't it?"

"I need to be getting along, sir . . . "

"And your father needs good wood, of which I've plenty. Come inside for a moment, instead of standing there like a starved thing." He called over his shoulder, telling his wife to put the water on the fire.

Reluctantly Kathrin gathered her bags and followed Peter into his workshop. She blinked against the dusty air and removed her hat. Sawdust carpeted the floor, fine and golden in places, crisp and coiled in others, while a heady concoction of resins and glues filled the air. Pots simmered on fires. Wood was being steamed into curves, or straightened where it was curved. Many sharp tools gleamed on one wall, some of them fashioned with blades of skydrift. Wheels, mostly awaiting spokes or iron tires, rested against another. Had the wheels been sledges, it could have been her father's workshop, when he had been busier.

Peter showed Kathrin to an empty stool next to one of his benches. "Sit down here and take the weight off your feet. Mary can make you some bread and cheese. Or bread and ham if you'd rather."

"That's kind sir, but Widow Grayling normally gives me something to eat, when I reach her house."

Peter raised a white eyebrow. He stood by the bench with his thumbs tucked into the belt of his apron, his belly jutting out as if he was quietly proud of it. "I didn't know you visited the witch."

"She will have her two hog's heads, once a month, and her candles. She only buys them from the Shield, not the Town. She pays for the hogs a year in advance, twenty-four whole pounds."

"And you're not scared by her?"

"I've no cause to be."

"There's some that would disagree with you."

Remembering something her father had told her, Kathrin said, "There are folk who say the Sheriff can fly, or that there was once a bridge that winked at travelers like an eye, or a road of iron that reached all the way to London. My father says there's no reason for anyone to be scared of Widow Grayling."

"Not afraid she'll turn you into a toad, then?"

"She cures people, not put spells on them."

"When she's in the mood for it. From what I've heard she's just as likely to turn the sick and needy away."

"If she helps some people, isn't that better than nothing at all?"

"I suppose." She could tell Peter didn't agree, but he wasn't cross with her for arguing. "What does your father make of you visiting the witch, anyway?"

"He doesn't mind."

"No?" Peter asked, interestedly.

"When he was small, my dad cut his arm on a piece of skydrift that he found in the snow. He went to Widow Grayling and she made his arm better again by tying an eel around it. She didn't take any payment except the skydrift."

"Does your father still believe an eel can heal a wound?"

"He says he'll believe anything if it gets the job done."

"Wise man, that Brendan, a man after my own heart. Which reminds me." Peter ambled to another bench, pausing to stir one of his bubbling pots before gathering a bundle of sawn-off wooden sticks. He set them down in front of Kathrin on a scrap of cloth. "Off cuts," he explained. "But good seasoned beech, which'll never warp. No use to me, but I am sure your father will find use for them. Tell him that there's more, if he wishes to collect it."

"I haven't got any money for wood."

"I'd take none. Your father was always generous to me, when I was going through lean times." Peter scratched behind his ear. "Only fair, the way I see it."

"Thank you," Kathrin said doubtfully. "But I don't think I can carry the wood all the way home."

"Not with two hog's heads as well. But you can drop by when you've given the heads to Widow Grayling."

"Only I won't be coming back over the river," Kathrin said. "After I've crossed Twenty Arch Bridge, I'll go back along the south quayside and take the ferry at Jarrow."

Peter looked puzzled. "Why line the ferryman's pocket when you can cross the bridge for nowt?"

Kathrin shrugged easily. "I've got to visit someone on the Jarrow road, to settle an account."

"Then you'd better take the wood now, I suppose," Peter said.

Mary bustled in, carrying a small wooden tray laden with bread and ham. She was as plump and red as her husband, only shorter. Picking up the entire gist of the conversation in an instant, she said, "Don't be an oaf, Peter. The girl cannot carry all that wood *and* her bags. If she will not come back this way, she must pass a message onto her father. Tell him that there's wood here if he wants it." She shook her head sympathetically at Kathrin. "What does he think you are, a pack mule?"

"I'll tell my father about the wood," she said.

"Seasoned beech," Peter said emphatically. "Remember that."

"I will."

Mary encouraged her to take some of the bread and meat, despite Kathrin again mentioning that she expected to be fed at Widow Grayling's. "Take it anyway," Mary said. "You never know how hungry you might get on the way home. Are you sure about not coming back this way?"

"I'd best not," Kathrin said.

After an awkward lull, Peter said, "There is something else I meant to tell your father. Could you let him know that I've no need of a new sledge this year, after all?"

"Peter," Mary said. "You promised."

"I said that I should *probably* need one. I was wrong in that." Peter looked exasperated. "The fault lies in Brendan, not me! If he did not make such good and solid sledges, then perhaps I should need another by now."

"I shall tell him," Kathrin said.

"Is your father keeping busy?" Mary asked.

"Aye," Kathrin answered, hoping the wheelwright's wife wouldn't push her on the point.

"Of course he will still be busy," Peter said, helping himself to some of the bread. "People don't stop needing sledges, just because the Great Winter loosens its hold on us. Any more than they stopped needing wheels when the winter was at its coldest. It's still cold for half the year!"

Kathrin opened her mouth to speak. She meant to tell Peter that he could pass the message onto her father directly, for he was working not five minutes walk from the wheelwright's shop. Peter clearly had no knowledge that her father had left the village, leaving his workshop empty during these warming months. But she realized that her father would be ashamed if the wheelwright were to learn of his present trade. It was best that nothing be said.

"Kathrin?" Peter asked.

"I should be getting on. Thank you for the food, and the offer of the wood."

"You pass our regards onto your father," Mary said.

"I shall."

"God go with you. Watch out for the jangling men."

"I will," Kathrin replied, because that was what you were supposed to say.

"Before you go," Peter said suddenly, as if a point had just occurred to him. "Let me tell you something. You say there are people who believe the Sheriff can fly, as if that was a foolish thing, like the iron road and the winking bridge. I cannot speak of the other things, but when I was boy I met someone who had seen the Sheriff's flying machine. My grandfather often spoke of it. A whirling thing, like a windmill made of tin. He had seen it when he was a boy, carrying the Sheriff and his men above the land faster than any bird."

"If the Sheriff could fly then, why does he need a horse and carriage now?"

"Because the flying machine crashed down to Earth, and no tradesman could persuade it to fly again. It was a thing of the old world, before the Great Winter. Perhaps the winking bridge and the iron road were also things of the old world. We mock too easily, as if we understood everything of our world where our forebears understood nothing."

"But if I should believe in certain things," Kathrin said, "should I not also believe in others? If the Sheriff can fly, then can a jangling man not steal me from my bed at night?"

"The jangling men are a story to stop children misbehaving," Peter said witheringly. "How old are you now?"

"Sixteen," Kathrin answered.

"I am speaking of something that was seen, in daylight, not made up to frighten bairns."

"But people say they have seen jangling men. They have seen men made of tin and gears, like the inside of a clock."

"Some people were frightened too much when they were small," Peter said, with a dismissive shake. "No more than that. But the Sheriff is real, and he was once able to fly. That's God's truth."

Her hands were hurting again by the time she reached Twenty Arch Bridge. She tugged down the sleeves of her sweater, using them as mittens. Rooks and jackdaws wheeled and cawed overhead. Seagulls feasted on waste floating in the narrow races between the bridge's feet, or pecked at vile leavings on the road that had been missed by the night soil gatherers. A boy laughed as Kathrin nearly tripped on the labyrinth of criss-crossing ruts that had been etched by years of wagon wheels entering and leaving the bridge. She hissed a curse back at the boy, but now the wagons served her purpose. She skulked near a doorway until a heavy cart came rumbling along, top-heavy with beer barrels from the Blue Star Brewery, drawn by four snorting dray-horses, a bored-looking drayman at the reins, huddled so down deep into his leather coat that it seemed as if the Great Winter still had its icy hand on the country.

Kathrin started walking as the cart lumbered past her, using it as a screen. Between the stacked beer barrels she could see the top level of the scaffolding that was shoring up the other side of the arch, visible since no house or parapet stood on that part of the bridge. A dozen or so workers—including a couple of aproned foremen—were standing on the scaffolding, looking down at the work going on below. Some of them had plumb lines; one of them even had a little black rod that shone a fierce red spot wherever he wanted something moved. Of Garret, the reason she wished to cross the bridge only once if she could help it, there was nothing to be seen. Kathrin hoped that he was under the side of the bridge, hectoring the workers. She felt sure that her father was down there too, being told what to do and biting his tongue against answering back. He put up with being shouted at, he put up with being forced to treat wood with crude disrespect, because it was all he could do to earn enough money to feed and shelter himself and his daughter. And he never, ever, looked Garret Kinnear in the eye.

Kathrin felt her mood easing as the dray ambled across the bridge, nearing the slight rise over the narrow middle arches. The repair work, where Garret was most likely to be, was now well behind her. She judged her progress by the passage of alehouses. She had passed the newly painted Bridge Inn and the shuttered gloom of the Lord's Confessor. Fiddle music spilled from the open doorway of the Dancing Panda: an old folksong with nonsense lyrics about *sickly sausage rolls.*

Ahead lay the Winged Man, its sign containing a strange painting of a foreboding figure rising from a hilltop. If she passed the Winged Man, she felt she would be safe.

Then the dray hit a jutting cobblestone and rightmost front wheel snapped free of its axle. The wheel wobbled off on its own. The cart tipped to the side, spilling beer barrels onto the ground. Kathrin stepped nimbly aside as one of the barrels ruptured and sent its fizzing, piss-colored contents across the roadway. The horses snorted and strained. The drayman spat out a greasy wad of chewing tobacco and started down from his chair, his face a mask of impassive resignation, as if this was the kind of thing that could be expected to happen once a day. Kathrin heard him whisper something in the ear of one of the horses, in beast-tongue, which calmed the animal.

Kathrin knew that she had no choice but to continue. Yet she had no sooner resumed her pace—moving faster now, the bags swaying awkwardly, than she saw Garret Kinnear. He was just stepping out of the Winged Man's doorway.

He smiled. "You in a hurry or something?"

Kathrin tightened her grip on the bags, as if she was going to use them as weapons. She decided not to say anything, not to openly acknowledge his presence, even though their eyes had met for an electric instant.

"Getting to be a big strong girl now, Kathrin Lynch."

She carried on walking, each step taking an eternity. How foolish she had been, to take Twenty Arch Bridge when it would only have cost her another hour to take the further crossing. She should not have allowed Peter to delay her with his good intentions.

"You want some help with them bags of yours?"

Out of the corner of her eye she saw him move out of the doorway, tugging his mud-stained trousers higher onto his hip. Garret Kinnear was snake thin, all skin and bone, but much stronger than he looked. He wiped a hand across his sharp beardless chin. He had long black hair, the greasy grey color of dishwater.

"Go away," she hissed, hating herself in the same instant.

"Just making conversation," he said.

Kathrin quickened her pace, glancing nervously around. All of a sudden the bridge appeared deserted. The shops and houses she had yet to pass were all shuttered and silent. There was still a commotion going on by the dray, but no one there was paying any attention to what was happening further along the bridge.

"Leave me alone," Kathrin said.

He was walking almost alongside her now, between Kathrin and the road. "Now what kind of way to talk is that, Kathrin Lynch? Especially after my offer to help you with them bags. What have you got in them, anyways?"

"Nothing that's any business of yours."

"I could be the judge of that." Before she could do anything, he'd snatched the bag from her left hand. He peered into its dark depths, frowning. "You came all the way from Jarrow Ferry with this?"

"Give me back the bag."

She reached for the bag, tried to grab it back, but he held it out of her reach, grinning cruelly.

"That's mine."

"How much would a pig's head be worth?"

"You tell me. There's only one pig around here."

They'd passed the mill next to the Winged Man. There was a gap between the mill and the six-storey house next to it, where some improbably narrow property must once have existed. Garret turned down the alley, still carrying Kathrin's bag. He reached the parapet at the edge of the bridge and looked over the side. He rummaged in the bag and drew out the pig's head. Kathrin hesitated at the entrance to the narrow alley, watching as Garret held the head out over the roiling water.

"You can have your pig back. Just come a wee bit closer."

"So you can do what you did last time?"

"I don't remember any complaints." He let the head fall, then caught it again, Kathrin's heart in her throat.

71

"You know I couldn't complain."

"Not much to ask for a pig's head, is it?" With his free hand, he fumbled open his trousers, tugging out the pale worm of his cock. "You did it before, and it didn't kill you. Why not now? I won't trouble you again."

She watched his cock stiffen. "You said that last time."

"Aye, but this time I mean it. Come over here, Kathrin. Be a good girl now and you'll have your pig back."

Kathrin looked back over her shoulder. No one was going to disturb them. The dray had blocked all the traffic behind it, and nothing was coming over the bridge from the south.

"Please," she said.

"Just this once," Garret said. "And make your mind up fast, girl. This pig's getting awfully heavy in my hand."

Kathrin stood in the widow's candlelit kitchen—it only had one tiny, dusty window - while the old woman turned her bent back to attend to the coals burning in her black metal stove. She poked and prodded the fire until it hissed back like a cat. "You came all the way from Jarrow Ferry?" she asked.

"Aye," Kathrin said. The room smelled smoky.

"That's too far for anyone, let alone a sixteen year old lass. I should have a word with your father. I heard he was working on Twenty Arch Bridge."

Kathrin shifted uncomfortably. "I don't mind walking. The weather's all right."

"So they say. All the same, the evenings are still cold, and there are types about you wouldn't care to meet on your own, miles from Jarrow."

"I'll be back before it gets dark," Kathrin said, with more optimism than she felt. Not if she went out of her way to avoid Garret Kinnear she wouldn't. He knew the route she'd normally take back home, and the alternatives would mean a much longer journey.

"You sure about that?"

"I have no one else to visit. I can start home now." Kathrin offered her one remaining bag, as Widow Grayling turned from the fire, brushing her hands on her apron.

"Put it on the table, will you?"

Kathrin put the bag down. "One pig's head, and twenty candles, just as you wanted," she said brightly.

Widow Grayling hobbled over to the table, supporting herself with a stick, eyeing Kathrin as she opened the bag and took out the solitary head. She weighed it in her hand then set it down on the table, the head facing Kathrin in such a way that its beady black eyes and smiling snout suggested amused complicity.

"It's a good head," the widow said. "But there were meant to be two of them."

"Can you manage with just the one, until I visit again? I'll have three for you next time."

"I'll manage if I must. Was there a problem with the butcher in the Shield?"

Kathrin had considered feigning ignorance, saying that she did not recall how only one head had come to be in her bags. But she knew Widow Grayling too well for that.

"Do you mind if I sit down?"

"Of course." The widow hobbled around the table to one of the rickety stools and dragged it out. "Are you all right, girl?"

Kathrin lowered herself onto the stool.

"The other bag was taken from me," she answered quietly.

"By who?"

"Someone on the bridge."

"Children?"

"A man."

Widow Grayling nodded slowly, as if Kathrin's answer had only confirmed some deep-seated suspicion she had harbored for many years. "Thomas Kinnear's boy, was it?"

"How could you know?"

"Because I've lived long enough to form ready opinions of people. Garret Kinnear is filth. But there's no one that'll touch him, because they're scared of his father. Even the Sheriff tugs his forelock to Thomas Kinnear. Did he rape you?"

"No. But he wanted me to do something nearly as bad."

"And did he make you?"

Kathrin looked away.

"Not this time."

Widow Grayling closed her eyes. She reached across the table and took one of Kathrin's hands, squeezing it between her own. "When was it?"

"Three months ago, when there was still snow on the ground. I had to cross the bridge on my own. It was later than usual, and there weren't any people around. I knew about Garret already, but I'd managed to keep away from him. I thought I was going to be lucky." Kathrin turned back to face her companion. "He caught me and took me into one of

73

the mills. The wheels were turning, but there was nobody inside except me and Garret. I struggled, but then he put his finger to my lips and told me to shush."

"Because of your father."

"If I made trouble, if I did not do what he wanted, Garret would tell his father some lie about mine. He would say that he caught him sleeping on the job, or drunk, or stealing nails."

"Garret promised you that?"

"He said, life's hard enough for a sledge-maker's daughter when no one wants sledges. He said it would only be harder if my father lost his work."

"In that respect he was probably right," the widow said resignedly. "It was brave of you to hold your silence, Kathrin. But the problem hasn't gone away, has it? You cannot avoid Garret forever."

"I can take the other bridge."

"That'll make no difference, now that he has his eye on you."

Kathrin looked down at her hands. "Then he's won already."

"No, he just thinks that he has." Without warning the widow stood from her chair. "How long have we known each other, would you say?"

"Since I was small."

"And in all that time, have I come to seem any older to you?"

"You've always seemed the same to me, Widow Lynch."

"An old woman. The witch on the hill."

"There are good witches and bad witches," Kathrin pointed out.

"And there are mad old women who don't belong in either category. Wait a moment."

Widow Grayling stooped under the impossibly low doorway into the next room. Kathrin heard a scrape of wood on wood, as of a drawer being opened. She heard rummaging sounds. Widow Grayling returned with something in her hands, wrapped in red cotton. Whatever it was, she put it down on the table. By the noise it made Kathrin judged that it was an item of some weight and solidity.

"I was just like you once. I grew up not far from Ferry, in the darkest, coldest years of the Great Winter."

"How long ago?"

"The Sheriff then was William the Questioner. You won't have heard of him." Widow Grayling sat down in the same seat she'd been using before and quickly exposed the contents of the red cotton bundle.

Kathrin wasn't quite sure what she was looking at. There was a thick and unornamented bracelet, made of some dull grey metal like pewter. Next to the ornament was something like the handle of a broken sword: a grip, with a crissed-crossed pattern on it, with a curved guard reaching from one end of the hilt to the other. It was fashioned from the same dull grey metal.

"Pick it up," the widow said. "Feel it."

Kathrin reached out tentatively and closed her finger around the criss-crossed hilt. It felt cold and hard and not quite the right shape for her hand. She lifted it from the table, feeling its weight.

"What is it, widow?"

"It's yours. It's a thing that has been in my possession for a very long while, but now it must change hands."

Kathrin didn't know quite what to say. A gift was a gift, but neither she nor her father would have any use for this ugly broken thing, save for its value to a scrap man.

"What happened to the sword?" she asked.

"There was never a sword. The thing you are holding is the entire object."

"Then I don't understand what it is for."

"You shall, in time. I'm about to place a hard burden on your shoulders. I have often thought that you were the right one, but I wished to wait until you were older, stronger. But what has happened today cannot be ignored. I am old and weakening. It would be a mistake to wait another year."

"I still don't understand."

"Take the bracelet. Put it on your wrist."

Kathrin did as she was told. The bracelet opened on a heavy hinge, like a manacle. When she locked it together, the join was nearly invisible. It was a cunning thing, to be sure. But it still felt as heavy and dead and useless as the broken sword.

Kathrin tried to keep a composed face, while all the while suspecting that the widow was as mad as people had always said.

"Thank you," she said, with as much sincerity as she could muster.

"Now listen to what I have to say. You walked across the bridge today. Doubtless you passed the inn known as the Winged Man."

"It was where Garret caught up with me."

"Did it ever occur to you to wonder where the name of the tavern comes from?"

"My dad told me once. He said the tavern was named after a metal statue that used to stand on a hill to the south, on the Durham road."

"And did your father explain the origin of this statue?"

"He said some people reckoned it had been up there since before the Great Winter. Other people said an old sheriff had put it up. Some other people . . . " But Kathrin trailed off.

"Yes?"

"It's silly, but they said a real Winged Man had come down, out of the sky."

"And did your father place any credence in that story?"

"Not really," Kathrin said.

"He was right not to. The statue was indeed older than the Great Winter, when they tore it down. It was not put up to honor the sheriff, or commemorate the arrival of a Winged Man." Now the widow looked at her intently. "But a Winged Man *did* come down. I know what happened, Kathrin: I saw the statue with my own eyes, before the Winged Man fell. I was there."

Kathrin shifted. She was growing uncomfortable in the widow's presence.

"My dad said people reckoned the Winged Man came down hundreds of years ago."

"It did."

"Then you can't have been there, Widow Grayling."

"Because if I had been, I should be dead by now? You're right. By all that is natural, I should be. I was born three hundred years ago, Kathrin. I've been a widow for more than two hundred of those years, though not always under this name. I've moved from house to house, village to village, as soon as people start suspecting what I am. I found the Winged Man when I was sixteen years old, just like you."

Kathrin smiled tightly. "I want to believe you."

"You will, shortly. I already told you that this was the coldest time of the Great Winter. The sun was a cold grey disk, as if it was made of ice itself. For years the river hardly thawed at all. The Frost Fair stayed almost all year round. It was nothing like the miserable little gatherings you have known. This was ten times bigger, a whole city built on the frozen river. It had streets and avenues, its own quarters. There were tents and stalls, with skaters and sledges everywhere. There'd be races, jousting competitions, fireworks, mystery players, even printing presses to make newspapers and souvenirs just for the Frost Fair. People came from miles around to see it, Kathrin: from as far away as Carlisle or York."

"Didn't they get bored with it, if it was always there?"

"It was always changing, though. Every few months there was something different. You would travel fifty miles to see a new wonder if enough people started talking about it. And there was no shortage of wonders, even if they were not always quite what you had imagined when you set off on your journey. Things fell from the sky more often in those days. A living thing like the Winged Man was still a rarity, but other things came down regularly enough. People would spy where they fell and try to get there first. Usually all they'd find would be bits of hot metal, all warped and runny like melted sugar."

"Skydrift," Kathrin said. "Metal that's no use to anyone, except barbers and butchers."

"Only because we can't make fires hot enough to make that metal smelt down like iron or copper. Once, we could. But if you could find a small piece with an edge, there was *nothing* it couldn't cut through. A surgeon's best knife will always be skydrift."

"Some people think the metal belongs to the jangling men, and that anyone who touches it will be cursed."

"And I'm sure the sheriff does nothing to persuade them otherwise. Do you think the jangling men care what happens to their metal?"

"I don't think they care, because I don't think they exist."

"I was once of the same opinion. Then something happened to make me change my mind."

"This being when you found the Winged Man, I take it."

"Before even that. I would have been thirteen, I suppose. It was in the back of a tent in the Frost Fair. There was a case holding a hand made of metal, found among skydrift near Wallsend."

"A rider's gauntlet."

"I don't think so. It was broken off at the wrist, but you could tell that it used to belong to something that was also made of metal. There were metal bones and muscles in it. No cogs or springs, like in a clock or tin toy. This was something finer, more ingenious. I don't believe any man could have made it. But it cannot just be the jangling men who drop things from the sky, or fall out of it."

"Why not?" Kathrin asked, in the spirit of someone going along with a game.

"Because it was said that the sheriff's men once found a head of skin and bone, all burned up, but which still had a pair of spectacles on it. The glass in them was dark like coal, but when the sheriff wore them, he could see at night like a wolf. Another time, his men found a shred of garment that kept changing color, depending on what it was lying against. You could hardly see it then. Not enough to make a suit, but you could imagine how useful that would have been to the sheriff's spies."

"They'd have wanted to get to the Winged Man first."

Widow Grayling nodded. "It was just luck that I got to him first. I was on the Durham road, riding a mule, when he fell from the sky. Now, the law said that they would spike your head on the bridge if you touched something that fell on the Sheriff's land, especially skydrift.

But everyone knew that the Sheriff could only travel so fast, even when he had his flying machine. It was a risk worth taking, so I took it, and I found the Winged Man, and he was still alive."

"Was he really a man?"

"He was a creature of flesh and blood, not a jangling man, but he was not like any man I had seen before. He was smashed and bent, like a toy that had been trodden on. When I found him he was covered in armor, hot enough to turn the snow to water and make the water hiss and bubble under him. I could only see his face. A kind of golden mask had come off, lying next to him. There were bars across his mask, like the head of the Angel on the tavern sign. The rest of him was covered in metal, jointed in a clever fashion. It was silver in places and black in others, where it had been scorched. His arms were metal wings, as wide across as the road itself if they had not been snapped back on themselves. Instead of legs he just had a long tail, with a kind of fluke at the end of it. I crept closer, watching the sky all around me for the sheriff's whirling machine. I was fearful at first, but when I saw the Winged Man's face I only wanted to do what I could for him. And he was dying. I knew it, because I'd seen the same look on the faces of men hanging from the sheriff's killing poles."

"Did you talk to him?"

"I asked him if he wanted some water. At first he just looked at me, his eyes pale as the sky, his lips opening and closing like a fish that has just been landed. Then he said 'Water will not help me.' Just those five words, in a dialect I didn't know. Then I asked him if there was anything else I could do to help him, all the while glancing over my shoulder in case anyone should come upon us. But the road was empty and the sky was clear. It took a long time for him to answer me again."

"What did he say?"

"He said 'Thank you, but there is nothing you can do for me.' Then I asked him if he was an angel. He smiled, ever so slightly. 'No,' he said. 'Not an angel, really. But I am a flier.' I asked him if there was a difference. He smiled again before answering me. 'Perhaps not, after all this time. Do you know of fliers, girl? Do any of you still remember the war?' "

"What did you tell him?"

"The truth. I said I knew nothing of a war, unless he spoke of the Battle of the Stadium of Light, which had only happened twenty years earlier. He looked sad, then, as if he had hoped for a different answer. I asked him if he was a kind of soldier. He said that he was. 'Fliers are warriors', he said. 'Men like me are fighting a great war, on your behalf, against an enemy you do not even remember.' "

"What enemy?"

"The jangling men. They exist, but not in the way we imagine them. They don't crawl in through bedroom windows at night, clacking tin-bodied things with skull faces and clockwork keys whirring from their backs. But they're real enough."

"Why would such things exist?"

"They'd been made to do the work of men on the other side of the sky, where men cannot breathe because the air is so thin. They made the jangling men canny enough that they could work without being told *exactly* what to do. But that already made them slyer than foxes. The jangling men coveted our world for themselves. That was before the Great Winter came in. The flier said that men like him—special soldiers, born and bred to fight the jangling men—were all that was holding them back."

"And he told you they were fighting a war, above the sky?"

Something pained Widow Grayling. "All the years since haven't made it any easier to understand what the flier told me. He said that, just as there may be holes in a old piece of timber, one that has been eaten through by woodworm, so there may be holes in the sky itself. He said that his wings were not really to help him fly, but to help him navigate those tunnels in the sky, just as the wheels of a cart find their way into the ruts on a road."

"I don't understand. How can there be holes in the sky, when the air is already too thin to breathe?"

"He said that the fliers and the jangling men make these holes, just as armies may dig a shifting network of trenches and tunnels as part of a long campaign. It requires strength to dig a hole and more strength to shore it up when it has already been dug. In an army, it would be the muscle of men and horses and whatever machines still work. But the flier was talking about a different kind of strength altogether." The widow paused, then stared into Kathrin's eyes with a look of foreboding. "He told me where it came from, you see. And ever since then, I have seen the world with different eyes. It is a hard burden, Kathrin. But someone must bear it."

Without thinking, Kathrin said, "Tell me."

"Are you sure?"

"Yes. I want to know."

"That bracelet has been on your wrist for a few minutes now. Does it feel any different?"

"No," Kathrin said automatically, but as soon as she'd spoken, as soon as she'd moved her arm, she knew that it was not the case. The bracelet still looked the same, it still looked like a lump of cold dead metal, but it seemed to hang less heavily against her skin than when she'd first put it on.

"The flier gave it to me," Widow Grayling said, observing Kathrin's reaction. "He told me how to open his armor and find the bracelet. I asked why. He said it was because I had offered him water. He was giving me something in return for that kindness. He said that the bracelet would keep me healthy, make me strong in other ways, and that if anyone else was to wear it, it would cure them of many ailments. He said that it was against the common law of his people to give such a gift to one such as I, but he chose to do it anyway. I opened his armor, as he told me, and I found his arm, bound by iron straps to the inside of his wing, and broken like the wing itself. On the end of his arm was this bracelet."

"If the bracelet had the power of healing, why was the Winged Man dying?"

"He said that there were certain afflictions it could not cure. He had been touched by the poisonous ichor of a jangling man, and the bracelet could do nothing for him now."

"I still do not believe in magic," Kathrin said carefully.

"Certain magics are real, though. The magic that makes a machine fly, or a man see in the dark. The bracelet feels lighter, because part of it has entered you. It is in your blood now, in your marrow, just as the jangling man's ichor was in the flier's. You felt nothing, and you will continue to feel nothing. But so long as you wear the bracelet, you will age much slower than anyone else. For centuries, no sickness or infirmity will touch you."

Kathrin stroked the bracelet. "I do not believe this."

"I would not expect to you. In a year or two, you will feel no change in yourself. But in five years, or in ten, people will start to remark upon your uncommon youthfulness. For a while, you will glory in it. Then you will feel admiration turn slowly to envy and then to hate, and it will start to feel like a curse. Like me, you will need to move on and take another name. This will be the pattern of your life, while your wear the flier's charm."

Kathrin looked at the palms of her hand. It might have been imagination, but the lines where the handles had cut into her were paler and less sensitive to the touch.

"Is this how you heal people?" she asked.

"You're as wise as I always guessed you were, Kathrin Lynch. Should you come upon someone who is ill, you need only place the bracelet around their wrist for a whole day and—unless they have the jangling man's ichor in them - they will be cured."

"What of the other things? When my father hurt his arm, he said you tied an eel around his arm."

Her words made the widow smile. "I probably did. I could just as well have smeared pigeon dung on it instead, or made him wear a necklace of worms, for all the difference it would have made. Your father's arm would have mended itself on its own, Kathrin. The cut was deep, but clean. It did not need the bracelet to heal, and your father was neither stupid nor feverish. But he did have the loose tongue of all small boys. He would have seen the bracelet, and spoken of it."

"Then you did nothing."

"Your father believed that I did something. That was enough to ease the pain in his arm and perhaps allow it to heal faster than it would otherwise have done."

"But you turn people away."

"If they are seriously ill, but neither feverish nor unconscious, I cannot let them see the bracelet. There is no other way, Kathrin. Some must die, so that the bracelet's secret is protected."

"This is the burden?" Kathrin asked doubtfully.

"No, this is the reward for carrying the burden. The burden is knowledge."

Again, Kathrin said, "Tell me."

"This is what the flier told me. The Great Winter fell across our world because the sun itself grew colder and paler. There was a reason for that. The armies of the celestial war were mining its fire, using the furnace of the sun itself to dig and shore up those seams in the sky. How they did this is beyond my comprehension, and perhaps even that of the flier himself. But he did make one thing clear. So long as the Great Winter held, the celestial war must still be raging. And that would mean that the jangling men had not yet won."

"But the Thaw . . . " Kathrin began.

"Yes, you see it now. The snow melts from the land. Rivers flow, crops grow again. The people rejoice, they grow stronger and happier, skins darken, the Frost Fairs fade into memory. But they do not understand what it really means."

Kathrin hardly dared ask. "Which side is winning, or has already won?"

"I don't know; that's the terrible part of it. But when the flier spoke to me, I sensed an awful hopelessness, as if he knew things were not going to go the way of his people."

"I'm frightened now."

"You should be. But someone needs to know, Kathrin, and the bracelet is losing its power to keep me out of the grave. Not because there is anything wrong with it, I think—it heals as well as it has ever done—but because it has decided that my time has grown sufficient, just as it will eventually decide the same thing with you."

Kathrin touched the other object, the thing that looked like a sword's handle.

"What is this?"

"The flier's weapon. His hand was holding it from inside the wing. It poked through the outside of the wing like the claw of a bat. The flier showed me how to remove it. It is yours as well."

She had touched it already, but this time Kathrin felt a sudden tingle as her fingers wrapped around the hilt. She let go suddenly, gasping as if she had reached for a stick and picked up an adder, squirming and slippery and venomous.

"Yes, you feel its power," Widow Grayling said admiringly. "It works for no one unless they carry the bracelet."

"I can't take it."

"Better you have it, than let that power go to waste. If the jangling men come, then at least someone will have a means to hurt them. Until then, there are other uses for it."

Without touching the hilt, Kathrin slipped the weapon into her pocket where it lay as heavy and solid as a pebble.

"Did you ever use it?"

"Once."

"What did you do?"

She caught a secretive smile on Widow Grayling's face. "I took something precious from William the Questioner. Banished him to the ground like the rest of us. I meant to kill him, but he was not riding in the machine when I brought it down."

Kathrin laughed. Had she not felt the power of the weapon, she might have dismissed the widow's story as the ramblings of an old woman. But she had no reason in the world to doubt her companion.

"You could have killed the sheriff later, when he came to inspect the killing poles."

"I nearly did. But something always stayed my hand. Then the sheriff was replaced by another man, and he in turn by another. Sheriffs came and went. Some were evil men, but not all of them. Some were only as hard and cruel as their office demanded. I never used the weapon again, Kathrin. I sensed that its power was not limitless, that it must be used sparingly, against the time when it became really necessary. But to use it in defense, against a smaller target . . . that would be a different matter, I think."

Kathrin thought she understood.

"I need to be getting back home," she said, trying to sound as if they had discussed nothing except the matter of the widow's next delivery of provisions. "I am sorry about the other head."

"There is no need to apologize. It was not your doing."

"What will happen to you now, widow?"

"I'll fade, slowly and gracefully. Perhaps I will see things through to the next winter. But I don't expect to see another thaw."

"Please. Take the bracelet back."

"Kathrin, listen. It will make no difference to me now, whether you take it or not."

"I'm not old enough for this. I'm only a girl from the Shield, a sledge-maker's daughter."

"What do you think I was, when I found the flier? We were the same. I've seen your strength and courage."

"I wasn't strong today."

"Yet you took the bridge, when you knew Garret would be on it. I have no doubt, Kathrin."

She stood. "If I had not lost the other head . . . if Garret had not caught me . . . would you have given me these things?"

"I was minded to do it. If not today, it would have happened next time. But let us give Garret due credit. He helped me make up my mind."

"He's still out there," Kathrin said.

"But he will know you will not be taking the bridge to get back home, even though that would save you paying the toll at Jarrow Ferry. He will content himself to wait until you cross his path again."

Kathrin collected her one remaining bag and moved to the door. "Yes."

"I will see you again, in a month. Give my regards to your father."

"I will."

Widow Grayling opened the door. The sky was darkening to the east, in the direction of Jarrow Ferry. The dusk stars would appear shortly, and it would be dark within the hour. The crows were still wheeling, but more languidly now, preparing to roost. Though the Great Winter was easing, the evenings seemed as cold as ever, as if night was the final stronghold, the place where the winter had retreated when the inevitability of its defeat became apparent. Kathrin knew that she would be shivering long before she reached the tollgate at the crossing, miles down the river. She tugged down her hat in readiness for the journey and stepped onto the broken road in front of the widow's cottage.

"You will take care now, Kathrin. Watch out for the janglies."

"I will, Widow Grayling."

The door closed behind her. She heard a bolt slide into place.

She was alone.

Kathrin set off, following the path she had used to climb up from the river. If it was arduous in daylight, it was steep and treacherous at dusk. As she descended she could see Twenty Arch Bridge from above, a thread of light across the shadowed ribbon of the river. Candles were being lit in the inns and houses that lined the bridge, tallow torches burning along the parapets. There was still light at the north end, where the sagging arch was being repaired. The obstruction caused by the dray had been cleared, and traffic was moving normally from bank to bank. She heard the calls of men and women, the barked orders of foremen, the braying of drunkards and slatterns, the regular creak and splash of the mill wheels turning under the arches.

Presently she reached a fork in the path and paused. To the right lay the quickest route down to the quayside road to Jarrow Ferry. To the left lay the easiest descent down to the bridge, the path that she had already climbed. Until that moment, her resolve had been clear. She would take the ferry, as she always did, as she was expected to do.

But now she reached a hand into her pocket and closed her fingers around the flier's weapon. The shiver of contact was less shocking this time. The object already felt a part of her, as if she had carried it for years.

She drew it out. It gleamed in twilight, shining where it had appeared dull before. Even if the widow had not told her of its nature, there would have been no doubt now. The object spoke its nature through her skin and bones, whispering to her on a level beneath language. It told her what it could do and how she could make it obey her. It told her to be careful of the power she now carried in her hand. She must scruple to use it wisely, for nothing like it now existed in the world. It was the power to smash walls. Power to smash bridges and towers and flying machines. Power to smash jangling men.

Power to smash ordinary men, if that was what she desired.

She had to know.

The last handful of crows gyred overhead. She raised the weapon to them and felt a sudden dizzying apprehension of their number and distance and position, each crow feeling distinct from its brethren, as if she could almost name them.

She selected one laggard bird. All the others faded from her attention, like players removing themselves from a stage. She came to know that last bird intimately. She could feel its wingbeats cutting the cold air. She could feel the soft thatch of its feathers, and the lacelike scaffolding of bone underneath. Within the cage of its chest she felt the tiny strong pulse of its heart, and she knew that she could make that heart freeze just by willing it.

The weapon seemed to urge her to do it. She came close. She came frighteningly close.

But the bird had done nothing to wrong her, and she spared it. She had no need to take a life to test this new gift, at least not an innocent one. The crow rejoined its brethren, something skittish and hurried in its flight, as if it had felt that coldness closing around its heart.

Kathrin returned the weapon to her pocket. She looked at the bridge again, measuring it once more with clinical eyes, eyes that were older and sadder this time, because she knew something that the people on the bridge could never know.

"I'm ready," she said, aloud, into the night, for whoever might be listening.

Then resumed her descent.

First published in *Interzone*, #209, April 2007.

ABOUT THE AUTHOR

A professional scientist with a Ph.D. in astronomy, **Alastair Reynolds** worked for the European Space Agency in the Netherlands for a number of years, but has recently moved back to his native Wales to become a full-time writer. His first novel, *Revelation Space,* was widely hailed as one of the major SF books of the year; it was quickly followed by *Chasm City, Redemption Ark, Absolution Gap, Century Rain,* and *Pushing Ice,* all big sprawling Space Operas that were big sellers as well, establishing Reynolds as one of the best and most popular new SF writers to enter the field in many years. His other books include a novella collection, *Diamond Dogs, Turquoise Days* and a chapbook novella, *The Six Directions of Space,* as well as three collections, *Galactic North, Zima Blue and Other Stories,* and *Deep Navigation.* His other novels include *The Prefect, House of Suns, Terminal World, Blue Remembered Earth, On the Steel Breeze, Terminal World,* and *Sleepover,* and a Doctor Who novel, *Harvest of Time.* Upcoming is a new book, *Slow Bullets.*

Tongtong's Summer
XIA JIA

Mom said to Tongtong, "In a couple of days, Grandpa is moving in with us."

After Grandma died, Grandpa lived by himself. Mom told Tongtong that because Grandpa had been working for the revolution all his life, he just couldn't be idle. Even though he was in his eighties, he still insisted on going to the clinic every day to see patients. A few days earlier, because it was raining, he had slipped on the way back from the clinic and hurt his leg.

Luckily, he had been rushed to the hospital, where they put a plaster cast on him. With a few more days of rest and recovery, he'd be ready to be discharged.

Emphasizing her words, Mom said, "Tongtong, your grandfather is old, and he's not always in a good mood. You're old enough to be considerate. Try not to add to his unhappiness, all right?"

Tongtong nodded, thinking, *But haven't I always been considerate?*

Grandpa's wheelchair was like a miniature electric car, with a tiny joystick by the armrest. Grandpa just had to give it a light push, and the wheelchair would glide smoothly in that direction. Tongtong thought it tremendous fun.

Ever since she could remember, Tongtong had been a bit afraid of Grandpa. He had a square face with long, white, bushy eyebrows that stuck out like stiff pine needles. She had never seen anyone with eyebrows that long.

She also had some trouble understanding him. Grandpa spoke Mandarin with a heavy accent from his native topolect. During dinner, when Mom explained to Grandpa that they needed to hire a caretaker for him, Grandpa kept on shaking his head emphatically and repeating: "Don't worry, eh!" Now Tongtong did understand *that* bit.

Back when Grandma had been ill, they had also hired a caretaker for her. The caretaker had been a lady from the countryside. She was short and small, but really strong. All by herself, she could lift Grandma—who had put on some weight—out of the bed, bathe her, put her on the toilet, and change her clothes. Tongtong had seen the caretaker lady accomplish these feats of strength with her own eyes. Later, after Grandma died, the lady didn't come any more.

After dinner, Tongtong turned on the video wall to play some games. *The world in the game is so different from the world around me,* she thought. In the game, a person just died. They didn't get sick, and they didn't sit in a wheelchair. Behind her, Mom and Grandpa continued to argue about the caretaker.

Dad walked over and said, "Tongtong, shut that off now, please. You've been playing too much. It'll ruin your eyes."

Imitating Grandpa, Tongtong shook her head and said, "Don't worry, eh!"

Mom and Dad both burst out laughing, but Grandpa didn't laugh at all. He sat stone-faced, with not even a hint of smile.

A few days later, Dad came home with a stupid-looking robot. The robot had a round head, long arms, and two white hands. Instead of feet it had a pair of wheels so that it could move forward and backward and spin around.

Dad pushed something in the back of the robot's head. The blank, smooth, egg-like orb blinked three times with a bluish light, and a young man's face appeared on the surface. The resolution was so good that it looked just like a real person.

"Wow," Tongtong said. "You are a robot?"

The face smiled. "Hello there! Ah Fu is my name."

"Can I touch you?"

"Sure!"

Tongtong put her hand against the smooth face, and then she felt the robot's arms and hands. Ah Fu's body was covered by a layer of soft silicone, which felt as warm as real skin.

Dad told Tongtong that Ah Fu was made by Guokr Technologies, Inc., and it was a prototype. Its biggest advantage was that it was as smart as a person: it knew how to peel an apple, how to pour a cup of tea, even how to cook, wash the dishes, embroider, write, play the piano . . . Anyway, having Ah Fu around meant that Grandpa would be given good care.

Grandpa sat there, still stone-faced, still saying nothing.

After lunch, Grandpa sat on the balcony to read the newspaper. He dozed off after a while. Ah Fu came over noiselessly, picked up Grandpa with his strong arms, carried him into the bedroom, set him down gently in bed, covered him with a blanket, pulled the curtains shut, and came out and shut the door, still not making any noise.

Tongtong followed Ah Fu and watched everything.

Ah Fu gave Tongtong's head a light pat. "Why don't you take a nap, too?"

Tongtong tilted her head and asked, "Are you really a robot?"

Ah Fu smiled. "Oh, you don't think so?"

Tongtong gazed at Ah Fu carefully. Then she said, very seriously, "I'm sure you are not."

"Why?"

"A robot wouldn't smile like that."

"You've never seen a smiling robot?"

"When a robot smiles, it looks scary. But your smile isn't scary. So you're definitely not a robot."

Ah Fu laughed. "Do you want to see what I really look like?"

Tongtong nodded. But her heart was pounding.

Ah Fu moved over by the video wall. From on top of his head, a beam of light shot out and projected a picture onto the wall. In the picture, Tongtong saw a man sitting in a messy room.

The man in the picture waved at Tongtong. Simultaneously, Ah Fu also waved in the exact same way. Tongtong examined the man in the picture: he wore a thin, grey, long-sleeved bodysuit, and a pair of grey gloves. The gloves were covered by many tiny lights. He also wore a set of huge goggles. The face behind the goggles was pale and thin, and looked just like Ah Fu's face.

Tongtong was stunned. "Oh, so you're the real Ah Fu!"

The man in the picture awkwardly scratched his head, and said, a little embarrassed, "Ah Fu is just the name we gave the robot. My real name is Wang. Why don't you call me Uncle Wang, since I'm a bit older?"

Uncle Wang told Tongtong that he was a fourth-year university student doing an internship at Guokr Technologies' R&D department. His group developed Ah Fu.

He explained that the aging population brought about serious social problems: many elders could not live independently, but their children had no time to devote to their care. Nursing homes made them feel lonely and cut off from society, and there was a lot of demand for trained, professional caretakers.

But if a home had an Ah Fu, things were a lot better. When not in use, Ah Fu could just sit there, out of the way. When it was needed, a request could be given, and an operator would come online to help the elder. This saved the time and cost of having caretakers commute to homes, and increased the efficiency and quality of care.

The Ah Fu they were looking at was a first-generation prototype. There were only three thousand of them in the whole country, being tested by three thousand families.

Uncle Wang told Tongtong that his own grandmother had also been ill and had to go to the hospital for an extended stay, so he had some experience with elder care. That was why he volunteered to come to her home to take care of Grandpa. As luck would have it, he was from the same region of the country as Grandpa, and could understand his topolect. A regular robot probably wouldn't be able to.

Uncle Wang laced his explanation with many technical words, and Tongtong wasn't sure she understood everything. But she thought the idea of Ah Fu splendid, almost like a science fiction story.

"So, does Grandpa know who you really are?"

"Your mom and dad know, but Grandpa doesn't know yet. Let's not tell him, for now. We'll let him know in a few days, after he's more used to Ah Fu."

Tongtong solemnly promised, "Don't worry, eh!"

She and Uncle Wang laughed together.

Grandpa really couldn't just stay home and be idle. He insisted that Ah Fu take him out walking. But after just one walk, he complained that it was too hot outside, and refused to go anymore.

Ah Fu told Tongtong in secret that it was because Grandpa felt self-conscious, having someone push him around in a wheelchair. He thought everyone in the street stared at him.

But Tongtong thought, *Maybe they were all staring at Ah Fu.*

Since Grandpa couldn't go out, being cooped up at home made his mood worse. His expression grew more depressed, and from time to time he burst out in temper tantrums. There were a few times when he screamed and yelled at Mom and Dad, but neither said anything. They just stood there and quietly bore his shouting.

But one time, Tongtong went to the kitchen and caught Mom hiding behind the door, crying.

Grandpa was now nothing like the Grandpa she remembered. It would have been so much better if he hadn't slipped and got hurt. Tongtong hated staying at home. The tension made her feel like she was suffocating. Every morning, she ran out the door, and would stay out until it was time for dinner.

Dad came up with a solution. He brought back another gadget made by Guokr Technologies: a pair of glasses. He handed the glasses to Tongtong and told her to put them on and walk around the house. Whatever she saw and heard was shown on the video wall.

"Tongtong, would you like to act as Grandpa's eyes?"

Tongtong agreed. She was curious about anything new.

Summer was Tongtong's favorite season. She could wear a skirt, eat watermelon and popsicles, go swimming, find cicada shells in the grass, splash through rain puddles in sandals, chase rainbows after a thunderstorm, get a cold shower after running around and working up a sweat, drink iced sour plum soup, catch tadpoles in ponds, pick grapes and figs, sit out in the backyard in the evenings and gaze at stars, hunt for crickets after dark with a flashlight . . . In a word: everything was wonderful in summer.

Tongtong put on her new glasses and went to play outside. The glasses were heavy and kept on slipping off her nose. She was afraid of dropping it.

Since the beginning of summer vacation, she and more than a dozen friends, both boys and girls, had been playing together every day. At their age, play had infinite variety. Having exhausted old games, they would invent new ones. If they were tired or too hot, they would go by the river and jump in like a plate of dumplings going into the pot. The sun blazed overhead, but the water in the river was refreshing and cool. This was heaven!

Someone suggested that they climb trees. There was a lofty pagoda tree by the river shore, whose trunk was so tall and thick that it resembled a dragon rising into the blue sky.

But Tongtong heard Grandpa's urgent voice by her ear: "Don't climb that tree! Too dangerous!"

Huh, so the glasses also act as a phone. Joyfully, she shouted back, "Grandpa, don't worry, eh!" Tongtong excelled at climbing trees. Even her father said that in a previous life she must have been a monkey.

But Grandpa would not let her alone. He kept on buzzing in her ear, and she couldn't understand a thing he was saying. It was getting on her nerves, so she took off the glasses and dropped them in the grass at the foot of the tree. She took off her sandals and began to climb, rising into the sky like a cloud.

This tree was easy. The dense branches reached out to her like hands, pulling her up. She went higher and higher and soon left her companions behind. She was about to reach the very top. The breeze whistled through the leaves, and sunlight dappled through the canopy. The world was so quiet.

She paused to take a breath, but then she heard her father's voice coming from a distance: "Tongtong, get . . . down . . . here . . . "

She poked her head out to look down. A little ant-like figure appeared far below. It really was Dad.

On the way back home, Dad really let her have it.

"How could you have been so foolish?! You climbed all the way up there by yourself. Don't you understand the risk?"

She knew that Grandpa told on her. Who else knew what she was doing?

She was livid. *He can't climb trees any more, and now he won't let others climb trees, either? So lame! And it was so embarrassing to have Dad show up and yell like that.*

The next morning, she left home super early again. But this time, she didn't wear the glasses.

"Grandpa was just worried about you," said Ah Fu. "If you fell and broke your leg, wouldn't you have to sit in a wheelchair, just like him?"

Tongtong pouted and refused to speak.

Ah Fu told her that through the glasses left at the foot of the tree, Grandpa could see that Tongtong was really high up. He was so worried that he screamed himself hoarse, and almost tumbled from his wheelchair.

But Tongtong remained angry with Grandpa. What was there to worry about? She had climbed plenty of trees taller than that one, and she had never once been hurt.

Since the glasses weren't being put to use, Dad packed them up and sent them back to Guokr. Grandpa was once again stuck at home with nothing to do. He somehow found an old Chinese Chess set and demanded Ah Fu play with him.

Tongtong didn't know how to play, so she pulled up a stool and sat next to the board just to check it out. She enjoyed watching Ah Fu pick up the old wooden pieces, their colors faded from age, with its slender, pale white fingers; she enjoyed watching it tap its fingers lightly on the table as it considered its moves. The robot's hand was so pretty, almost like it was carved out of ivory.

But after a few games, even she could tell that Ah Fu posed no challenge to Grandpa at all. A few moves later, Grandpa once again captured one of Ah Fu's pieces with a loud snap on the board.

"Oh, you suck at this," Grandpa muttered.

To be helpful, Tongtong also said, "You suck!"

"A real robot would have played better," Grandpa added. He had already found out the truth about Ah Fu and its operator.

Grandpa kept on winning, and after a few games, his mood improved. Not only did his face glow, but he was also moving his head about and humming folk tunes. Tongtong also felt happy, and her earlier anger at Grandpa dissipated.

Only Ah Fu wasn't so happy. "I think I need to find you a more challenging opponent," he said.

When Tongtong returned home, she almost jumped out of her skin. Grandpa had turned into a monster!

He was now dressed in a thin, grey, long-sleeved bodysuit, and a pair of grey gloves. Many tiny lights shone all over the gloves. He wore a set of huge goggles over his face, and he waved his hands about and gestured in the air.

On the video wall in front of him appeared another man, but not Uncle Wang. This man was as old as Grandpa, with a full head of silver-white hair. He wasn't wearing any goggles. In front of him was a Chinese Chess board.

"Tongtong, come say hi," said Grandpa. "This is Grandpa Zhao."

Grandpa Zhao was Grandpa's friend from back when they were in the army together. He had just had a heart stent put in. Like Grandpa, he was bored, and his family also got their own Ah Fu. He was also a Chinese Chess enthusiast, and complained about the skill level of his Ah Fu all day.

Uncle Wang had the inspiration of mailing telepresence equipment to Grandpa and then teaching him how to use it. And within a few days, Grandpa was proficient enough to be able to remotely control Grandpa Zhao's Ah Fu to play chess with him.

Not only could they play chess, but the two old men also got to chat with each other in their own native topolect. Grandpa became so joyous and excited that he seemed to Tongtong like a little kid.

"Watch this," said Grandpa.

He waved his hands in the air gently, and through the video wall, Grandpa Zhao's Ah Fu picked up the wooden chessboard, steady as you please, dexterously spun it around in the air, and set it back down without disturbing a piece.

Tongtong watched Grandpa's hands without blinking. *Are these the same unsteady, jerky hands that always made it hard for Grandpa to do anything?* It was even more amazing than magic.

"Can I try?" she asked.

Grandpa took off the gloves and helped Tongtong put them on. The gloves were stretchy, and weren't too loose on Tongtong's small hands. Tongtong tried to wiggle her fingers, and the Ah Fu in the video wall wiggled its fingers, too. The gloves provided internal resistance that steadied and smoothed out Tongtong's movements, and thus also the movements of Ah Fu.

Grandpa said, "Come, try shaking hands with Grandpa Zhao."

In the video, a smiling Grandpa Zhao extended his hand. Tongtong carefully reached out and shook hands. She could feel the subtle, immediate pressure changes within the glove, as if she were really shaking a person's hand—it even felt warm! *This is fantastic!*

Using the gloves, she directed Ah Fu to touch the chessboard, the pieces, and the steaming cup of tea next to them. Her fingertips felt the sudden heat from the cup. Startled, her fingers let go, and the cup fell to the ground and broke. The chessboard was flipped over, and chess pieces rolled all over the place.

"Aiya! Careful, Tongtong!"

"No worries! No worries!" Grandpa Zhao tried to get up to retrieve the broom and dustpan, but Grandpa told him to remain seated. "Careful about your hands!" Grandpa said. "I'll take care of it." He put on the gloves and directed Grandpa Zhao's Ah Fu to pick up the chess pieces one by one, and then swept the floor clean.

Grandpa wasn't mad at Tongtong, and didn't threaten to tell Dad about the accident she caused.

"She's just a kid, a bit impatient," he said to Grandpa Zhao. The two old men laughed.

Tongtong felt both relieved and a bit misunderstood.

Once again, Mom and Dad were arguing with Grandpa.

The argument went a bit differently from before. Grandpa was once again repeating over and over, "Don't worry, eh!" But Mom's tone grew more and more severe.

The actual point of the argument grew more confusing to Tongtong the more she listened. All she could make out was that it had something to do with Grandpa Zhao's heart stent.

In the end, Mom said, "What do you mean? 'Don't worry'? What if another accident happens? Would you please stop causing more trouble?"

Grandpa got so mad that he shut himself in his room and refused to come out, even for dinner.

Mom and Dad called Uncle Wang on the videophone. Finally, Tongtong figured out what happened.

Grandpa Zhao was playing chess with Grandpa, but the game got him so excited that his heart gave out—apparently, the stent wasn't put in perfectly. There had been no one else home at the time. Grandpa was the one who operated Ah Fu to give CPR to Grandpa Zhao, and also called an ambulance.

The emergency response team arrived in time and saved Grandpa Zhao's life.

What no one could have predicted was that Grandpa suggested that he go to the hospital to care for Grandpa Zhao—no, he didn't mean he'd go personally, but that they send Ah Fu over, and he'd operate Ah Fu from home.

But Grandpa himself needed a caretaker too. Who was supposed to care for the caretaker?

Further, Grandpa came up with the idea that when Grandpa Zhao recovered, he'd teach Grandpa Zhao how to operate the telepresence equipment. The two old men would be able to care for each other, and they would have no need of other caretakers.

Grandpa Zhao thought this was a great idea. But both families thought the plan absurd. Even Uncle Wang had to think about it for a while and then said, "Um . . . I have to report this situation to my supervisors."

Tongtong thought hard about this. Playing chess through Ah Fu was simple to understand. But caring for each other through Ah Fu? The more she thought about it, the more complicated it seemed. She was sympathetic to Uncle Wang's confusion.

Sigh, Grandpa is just like a little kid. He wouldn't listen to Mom and Dad at all.

Grandpa now stayed in his room all the time. At first, Tongtong thought he was still mad at her parents. But then, she found that the situation had changed completely.

Grandpa got really busy. Once again, he started seeing patients. No, he didn't go to the clinic; instead, using his telepresence kit, he was operating Ah Fus throughout the country and showing up in other elders' homes. He would listen to their complaints, feel their pulse, examine them, and write out prescriptions. He also wanted to give acupuncture treatments through Ah Fus, and to practice this skill, he operated his own Ah Fu to stick needles in himself!

Uncle Wang told Tongtong that Grandpa's innovation could transform the entire medical system. In the future, maybe patients no longer needed to go to the hospital and waste hours in waiting rooms. Doctors could just come to your home through an Ah Fu installed in each neighborhood.

Uncle Wang said that Guokr's R&D department had formed a dedicated task force to develop a specialized, improved model of Ah Fu for such medical telepresence applications, and they invited Grandpa onboard as a consultant. So Grandpa got even busier.

Since Grandpa's legs were not yet fully recovered, Uncle Wang was still caring for him. But they were working on developing a web-based system that would allow anyone with some idle time and interest in helping others to register to volunteer. Then the volunteers would be able to sign on to Ah Fus in homes across the country to take care of elders, children, patients, pets, and to help in other ways.

If the plan succeeded, it would be a step to bring about the kind of golden age envisioned by Confucius millennia ago: "And then men would care for all elders as if they were their own parents, love all children as if they were their own children. The aged would grow old and die in security; the youthful would have opportunities to contribute and prosper; and children would grow up under the guidance and protection of all. Widows, orphans, the disabled, the diseased—everyone would be cared for and loved."

Of course, such a plan had its risks: privacy and security, misuse of telepresence by criminals, malfunctions and accidents, just for starters. But since technological change was already here, it was best to face the consequences and guide them to desirable ends.

There were also developments that no one had anticipated.

Uncle Wang showed Tongtong lots of web videos: Ah Fus were shown doing all kinds of interesting things: cooking, taking care of children, fixing the plumbing and electric systems around the house, gardening, driving, playing tennis, even teaching children the arts of *go* and calligraphy and seal carving and *erhu* playing . . .

All of these Ah Fus were operated by elders who needed caretakers themselves, too. Some of them could no longer move about easily, but still had sharp eyes and ears and minds; some could no longer remember things easily, but they could still replicate the skills they had perfected in their youth; and most of them really had few physical problems, but were depressed and lonely. But now, with Ah Fu, everyone was out and about, *doing* things.

No one had imagined that Ah Fu could be put to all these uses. No one had thought that men and women in their seventies and eighties could still be so creative and imaginative.

Tongtong was especially impressed by a traditional folk music orchestra made up of more than a dozen Ah Fus. They congregated around a pond in a park and played enthusiastically and loudly. According to Uncle

Wang, this orchestra had become famous on the web. The operators behind the Ah Fus were men and women who had lost their eyesight, and so they called themselves "The Old Blinds."

"Tongtong," Uncle Wang said, "your grandfather has brought about a revolution."

Tongtong remembered that Mom had often mentioned that Grandpa was an old revolutionary. "He's been working for the revolution all his life; it's time for him to take a break." But wasn't Grandpa a doctor? When did he participate in a "revolution"? And just what kind of work was "working for the revolution" anyway? And why did he have to do it all his life?

Tongtong couldn't figure it out, but she thought "revolution" was a splendid thing. Grandpa now once again seemed like the Grandpa she had known.

Every day, Grandpa was full of energy and spirit. Whenever he had a few moments to himself, he preferred to sing a few lines of traditional folk opera:

Outside the camp, they've fired off the thundering cannon thrice,
And out of Tianbo House walks the woman who will protect her homeland.
The golden helmet sits securely over her silver-white hair,
The old iron-scaled war robe once again hangs on her shoulders.
Look at her battle banner, displaying proudly her name:
Mu Guiying, at fifty-three, you are going to war again!

Tongtong laughed. "But Grandpa, you're eighty-three!"

Grandpa chuckled. He stood and posed as if he were an ancient general holding a sword as he sat on his warhorse. His face glowed red with joy.

In another few days, Grandpa would be eighty-four.

Tongtong played by herself at home.

There were dishes of cooked food in the fridge. In the evening, Tongtong took them out, heated them up, and ate by herself. The evening air was heavy and humid, and the cicadas cried without cease.

The weather report said there would be thunderstorms.

A blue light flashed three times in a corner of the room. A figure moved out of the corner noiselessly: Ah Fu.

"Mom and Dad took Grandpa to the hospital. They haven't returned yet."

Ah Fu nodded. "Your mother sent me to remind you: don't forget to close the windows before it rains."

Together, the robot and the girl closed all the windows in the house. When the thunderstorm arrived, the raindrops struck against the windowpanes like drumbeats. The dark clouds were torn into pieces by the white and purple flashes of lightning, and then a bone-rattling thunder rolled overhead, making Tongtong's ears ring.

"You're not afraid of thunder?" asked Ah Fu.

"No. You?"

"I was afraid when I was little, but not now."

An important question came to Tongtong's mind: "Ah Fu, do you think everyone has to grow up?"

"I think so."

"And then what?"

"And then you grow old."

"And then?"

Ah Fu didn't respond.

They turned on the video wall to watch cartoons. It was Tongtong's favorite show: "Rainbow Bear Village." No matter how heavy it rained outside, the little bears of the village always lived together happily. Maybe everything else in the world was fake; maybe only the world of the little bears was real.

Gradually, Tongtong's eyelids grew heavy. The sound of rain had a hypnotic effect. She leaned against Ah Fu. Ah Fu picked her up in its arms, carried her into the bedroom, set her down gently in bed, covered her with a blanket, and pulled the curtains shut. Its hands were just like real hands, warm and soft.

Tongtong murmured, "Why isn't Grandpa back yet?"

"Sleep. When you wake up, Grandpa will be back."

Grandpa did not come back.

Mom and Dad returned. Both looked sad and tired.

But they got even busier. Every day, they had to leave the house and go somewhere. Tongtong stayed home by herself. She played games sometimes, and watched cartoons at other times. Ah Fu sometimes came over to cook for her.

A few days later, Mom called for Tongtong. "I have to talk to you."

Grandpa had a tumor in his head. The last time he fell was because the tumor pressed against a nerve. The doctor suggested surgery immediately.

Given Grandpa's age, surgery was very dangerous. But not operating would be even more dangerous. Mom and Dad and Grandpa had gone to several hospitals and gotten several other opinions, and after talking with each other over several nights, they decided that they had to operate.

The operation took a full day. The tumor was the size of an egg.

Grandpa remained in a coma after the operation.

Mom hugged Tongtong and sobbed. Her body trembled like a fish.

Tongtong hugged Mom back tightly. She looked and saw the white hairs mixed in with the black on her head. Everything seemed so unreal.

Tongtong went to the hospital with Mom.

It was so hot, and the sun so bright. Tongtong and Mom shared a parasol. In Mom's other hand was a thermos of bright red fruit juice taken from the fridge.

There were few pedestrians on the road. The cicadas continued their endless singing. The summer was almost over.

Inside the hospital, the air conditioning was turned up high. They waited in the hallway for a bit before a nurse came to tell them that Grandpa was awake. Mom told Tongtong to go in first.

Grandpa looked like a stranger. His hair had been shaved off, and his face was swollen. One eye was covered by a gauze bandage, and the other eye was closed. Tongtong held Grandpa's hand, and she was scared. She remembered Grandma. Like before, there were tubes and beeping machines all around.

The nurse said Grandpa's name. "Your granddaughter is here to see you."

Grandpa opened his eye and gazed at Tongtong. Tongtong moved, and the eye moved to follow her. But he couldn't speak or move.

The nurse whispered, "You can talk to your grandfather. He can hear you."

Tongtong didn't know what to say. She squeezed Grandpa's hand, and she could feel Grandpa squeezing back.

Grandpa! She called out in her mind. *Can you recognize me?*

His eyes followed Tongtong.

She finally found her voice. "Grandpa!"

Tears fell on the white sheets. The nurse tried to comfort her. "Don't cry! Your grandfather would feel so sad to see you cry."

Tongtong was taken out of the room, and she cried—tears streaming down her face like a little kid, but she didn't care who saw—in the hallway for a long time.

Ah Fu was leaving. Dad packed it up to mail it back to Guokr Technologies.

Uncle Wang explained that he had wanted to come in person to say goodbye to Tongtong and her family. But the city he lived in was very far away. At least it was easy to communicate over long distances now, and they could chat by video or phone in the future.

Tongtong was in her room, drawing. Ah Fu came over noiselessly. Tongtong had drawn many little bears on the paper, and colored them all different shades with crayons. Ah Fu looked at the pictures. One of the biggest bears was colored all the shades of the rainbow, and he wore a black eye patch so that only one eye showed.

"Who is this?" Ah Fu asked.

Tongtong didn't answer. She went on coloring, her heart set on giving every color in the world to the bear.

Ah Fu hugged Tongtong from behind. Its body trembled. Tongtong knew that Ah Fu was crying.

Uncle Wang sent a video message to Tongtong.

Tongtong, did you receive the package I sent you?

Inside the package was a fuzzy teddy bear. It was colored like the rainbow, with a black eye patch, leaving only one eye. It was just like the one Tongtong drew.

The bear is equipped with a telepresence kit and connected to the instruments at the hospital: his heartbeat, breath, pulse, body temperature. If the bear's eye is closed, that means your grandfather is asleep. If your grandfather is awake, the bear will open its eye.

Everything the bear sees and hears is projected onto the ceiling of the room at the hospital. You can talk to it, tell it stories, sing to it, and your grandfather will see and hear.

He can definitely hear and see. Even though he can't move his body, he's awake inside. So you must talk to the bear, play with it, and let it hear your laughter. Then your grandfather won't be alone.

Tongtong put her ear to the bear's chest: thump-thump. The heartbeat was slow and faint. The bear's chest was warm, rising and falling slowly with each breath. It was sleeping deeply.

Tongtong wanted to sleep, too. She put the bear in bed with her and covered it with a blanket. *When Grandpa is awake tomorrow,* she thought, *I'll bring him out to get some sun, to climb trees, to go to the park and listen to those grandpas and grandmas sing folk opera. The summer isn't over yet. There are so many fun things to do.*

"Grandpa, don't worry, eh!" she whispered. *When you wake up, everything will be all right.*

Author's Note:

I'd like to dedicate this story to my grandfather. August is when I composed this story, and it's also the anniversary of his passing. I will treasure the time I got to spend with him forever.

This story is also dedicated to all the grandmas and grandpas who, each morning, can be seen in the parks practicing taichi, twirling swords, singing opera, dancing, showing off their songbirds, painting, doing calligraphy, playing the accordion. You made me understand that living with an awareness of the closeness of death is nothing to be afraid of.

First published in *Upgraded,*
edited by Neil Clarke.

ABOUT THE AUTHOR

As an undergraduate, **Xia Jia** majored in Atmospheric Sciences at Peking University. She then entered the Film Studies Program at the Communication University of China, where she completed her Master's thesis: "A Study on Female Figures in Science Fiction Films." Recently, she obtained a Ph.D. in Comparative Literature and World Literature at Peking University, with "Chinese Science Fiction and Its Cultural Politics Since 1990⊠ as the topic of her dissertation. She now teaches at Xi'an Jiaotong University.

She has been publishing fiction since college in a variety of venues, including *Science Fiction World* and *Jiuzhou Fantasy*. Several of her stories have won the Galaxy Award, China's most prestigious science fiction award. In English translation, she has been published in *Clarkesworld* and *Upgraded*.

China Dreams: Contemporary Chinese Science Fiction

KEN LIU

China has a vibrant science fiction culture whose sheer size can sometimes surprise Western readers unfamiliar with it. For example, China's largest science fiction magazine, *Science Fiction World,* has a current monthly circulation figure of around 160,000 (this is down from a peak of around 300,000, but copies are often read by multiple people as many high school students purchase them at newsstands and share with friends).

In contrast, the latest overall circulation figures for the big American SF print magazines are 27,248 for *Analog,* 23,192 for *Asimov's,* and 10,678 for *The Magazine of Fantasy & Science Fiction.*[1] Besides genre-specific magazines, some Chinese literary magazines, such as *ZUI Found,* are also open to SFnal work, and through these markets, the much larger "mainstream" readership is also exposed to science fiction, both translated and native.

The new online publication *SF Comet,* which hosts a monthly flash fiction contest for invited Chinese and Western science fiction writers (Nancy Kress and Mike Resnick are two recent participants), distributes contest entries to readers via WeChat (a mobile messaging application/platform) and Sina Weibo (a Twitter work-alike).

Although the contest is barely a few months old, it already has thousands of subscribers because readers enjoy the challenge of matching the anonymized entries to the names of the participating authors and voting for their favorite story via WeChat. (I tried guessing the authors during the last couple of contests, and though I failed miserably, I really enjoyed this way of experiencing flash fiction.)

Western fandom is starting to pay attention to Chinese science fiction. Beijing's bid to host Worldcon, though it lost to Kansas City, nonetheless made waves at LonCon 3. However, until recently, few Chinese SF works are translated into English, making it hard for non-Chinese readers to appreciate them.

This situation is now being remedied to some degree. In recent years, Anglophone science fiction markets such as *Apex, Clarkesworld, F&SF, Interzone, Lightspeed,* and others have all published works translated from Chinese. In addition, academic journals such as *Renditions* and China-based English literary journals like *Pathlight* have also been publishing some excellent genre translations, though my impression is that few genre readers in the West are aware of them or have sought them out.[2]

Starting in November of 2014, Tor Books will publish English translations of Liu Cixin's *Three-Body* trilogy, which is China's best-selling hard scifi series. And *Clarkesworld* has recently announced a partnership with Storycom International Culture Communication Co., Ltd. to publish more Chinese SF stories in translation. In short, it is now at least possible for the interested Anglophone reader to read some of these works without knowing Chinese.

Thus, if you're curious about Chinese science fiction, instead of listening to me, a very valid choice is to simply skip to the end of this essay and read up on the works cited in the bibliography.

Whenever the topic of Chinese science fiction comes up, I often hear Anglophone readers ask: "How is Chinese science fiction different from science fiction written in English?"

I usually disappoint them by replying that the question is ill defined and there isn't a neat sound bite for an answer. Any broad literary classification tied to a culture—especially a culture as in flux and contested as China's—encompasses all the complexities and contradictions in that culture. Attempts to provide neat answers will only result in broad generalizations that are of little value or stereotypes that reaffirm existing prejudices.

Thus, I limit myself here to providing context and describing specific authors and works. The title of this essay is a play on President Xi Jingping's promotion of the "Chinese Dream" as a slogan for China's development. Science fiction is the literature of dreams, and dreams always say something about the dreamer, the dream interpreter, as well as the audience. When reading Chinese science fiction through translation, the reader must constantly keep in mind the multiple layers of interpretation that are at play.

To start with, I don't believe that "science fiction written in English" is a useful category for comparison (the fiction written in Singapore, the United Kingdom, and the United States, for example, are all quite different, and there are further divisions within and across such geographical boundaries).

Moreover, imagine asking a hundred different American authors and critics to characterize "American science fiction"—you'd hear a hundred different answers. The same is true of Chinese authors and critics, and Chinese science fiction.

Chinese science fiction has also undergone tremendous change over time. Over about a hundred years, it has moved from the late Qing Dynasty tales of technological optimism to the socialist utopias of the early years of the People's Republic, to being suppressed as "spiritual pollution" in the 1980s, to a revival in the last two decades that has blossomed into a self-contained, rich literary tradition.[3]

Conclusions and generalizations that might have once been true about Chinese science fiction are no longer true. And thus I limit myself to discussing only works from the last decade or so (and with a particular focus on works that have been translated so that the reader may seek out the works themselves instead of blindly trusting my summary).

China is also going through a massive social, cultural, and technological transformation involving more than a billion people of different ethnicities, cultures, classes, and ideological sympathies, and it is impossible for anyone, even people who are living through these upheavals, to claim to know the entire picture.

If one's knowledge of China is limited to Western media reports or the experience of being a tourist or expat, claiming to "understand" China is akin to a man who has caught a glimpse of a fuzzy spot through a drinking straw claiming to know what a leopard is. The fiction produced in China reflects the complexity of the environment.

This is all a rather long-winded way to say that I think anyone who confidently asserts a definitive characterization of "Chinese science fiction" is either a) an outsider who doesn't know what they're talking about; or b) someone who *does* know something, but is deliberately ignoring the contested nature of the subject and presenting their opinion as fact.

There is, in fact, a fairly vibrant body of academic scholarship about Chinese science fiction, with insightful and interesting commentary by scholars such as Mingwei Song and Nathaniel Isaacson. Panels on Chinese science fiction are quite common at academic conferences on comparative literature and Asian studies. However, my impression is that many (most?) genre readers, writers, and critics in fandom are not familiar with this body of work. The scholarly essays generally avoid the pitfalls I warn about and are nuanced and careful in their analysis. Readers seeking an informed opinion are urged to look up these works.

So, I will state that I do not consider myself an expert on Chinese science fiction. Although I have read a sizable number of works of Chinese SF and translated some of them from Chinese into English, I know enough only to know that I don't know much. I know enough to know that I need to study more, a lot more. And I know enough to know that there are no simple answers.

A popular way for Chinese fans to describe the contemporary Chinese science fiction scene is to say that there are three prominent, active writers who belong to an older generation, the so-called "Big Three" of Liu Cixin, Wang Jinkang, and Han Song. In addition, there is a generation of younger writers who have generally achieved fame with short fiction, though many have also started novel careers.

It's impossible to speak of contemporary Chinese science fiction without starting with Liu Cixin, who has been sometimes described as a "neo-classical" writer whose novels and short stories are compared to the works of Isaac Asimov or Arthur C. Clarke, but with a modern, "Chinese" sensibility. Liu has won China's most prestigious literary genre awards multiple times, and his masterpiece, the *Three-Body* trilogy (consisting of *The Three-Body Problem, The Dark Forest,* and *Death's End*), has been credited for single-handedly gaining Chinese science fiction respectability among the Chinese literary establishment. A massive work spanning the time from China's Cultural Revolution to the end of the universe, the trilogy describes an alien invasion of Earth triggered by a Mao-era METI project, and the consequent scattering of humanity to the stars. Liu's short fiction is similarly characterized by a grand imaginative scope, though he often roots his stories in the lives of China's ordinary citizens who live far from the big cities and have little wealth.

The other two writers, Wang Jinkang and Han Song, are quite different. Wang Jinkang's works are very much concerned with the intersection of science and ethics. His recent novel *The Ant Life,* for instance, features a young scientist who succeeds in creating a utopia by infecting the people of an isolated community with hormones extracted from ants to replace their selfish desires with altruistic ones directed to the good of the community as a whole. As one might imagine, this experiment backfires and unintended consequences come to dominate. Many of Wang's stories are infused with this flavor of sociological SF.

Han Song, on the other hand, focuses his acerbic wit on the "science fictional" excesses of modern development, particularly as manifested in China's breakneck rush toward "progress." His *High-Speed Rail,* for instance, uses China's high-speed train network as a postmodern metaphor to explore the rapid and grotesque devolution (or perhaps unmooring) of values in contemporary China through a series of surreal, dark, violent images.

In contrast to the Big Three, the younger writers of the new generation generally have done their best works so far only in short form (though this is changing). They make use of a variety of approaches and styles, and it's very difficult to generalize about them in any useful way.

For example, this group includes the "science fiction realism" of Chen Qiufan (a.k.a. Stanley Chan), whose "The Year of the Rat" describes the plight of unemployed Chinese college grads being drafted to fight genetically engineered rats. The story can be read as a satire on the inequities and dislocations caused by China's rapid development as well as providing a perspective on China's low-wage manufacturing sector that may be unfamiliar to Western readers.

Chen's debut novel, *The Waste Tide,* is a cyberpunk thriller set in China's e-waste processing hub. Its detailed worldbuilding and meticulous attention to technical rigor are further enriched by trenchant observations concerning the complex linguistic landscape of China's economically developed regions, where multiple topolects of Sinitic languages as well as English coexist and compete. This focus on linguistic topography should come as no surprise when one learns that Chen is fluent in Mandarin, Cantonese, Teochew, English, and once won Taiwan's prestigious Dragon Fantasy Award for having written a science fiction story in Classical Chinese (a feat akin to one of us writing a science fiction story in Anglo-Saxon and then winning a Nebula or Hugo for it).

Next, encounter the "porridge SF" of Xia Jia, whose dreamlike, layered images defy easy genre classifications. In "A Hundred Ghosts Parade Tonight," Xia's rich prose sketches a fantastic world of ghosts that turn out to be a futuristic, abandoned theme park of post-human cyborgs.

In "Spring Festival: Happiness, Anger, Love, Sorrow, Joy," Xia's near-future vignettes of Chinese traditions transformed by technology are punctuated by supernatural acts of resistance and rebellion. Besides a career as one of China's most popular science fiction authors, Xia is also an accomplished scholar (she holds a Ph.D. in comparative literature) and translator (she has translated works by Ray Bradbury, among others).

You'll also find the overt, wry political metaphors of Ma Boyong, whose "City of Silence" pays homage to *1984* by upgrading the machinery of state surveillance with network technology and counters it with acts of resistance drawn from the experience of Chinese netizens.

Incisive, funny, and erudite, Ma's works are deeply allusive, featuring surprising and entertaining juxtapositions of traditional elements from Chinese culture and history against contemporary references. The ease with which Ma marshals his encyclopedic knowledge of Chinese history and traditions also makes it a challenge to translate his most interesting works.

For example, he has written an imaginative history of coffee in China that applies the conventions of China's rich millennia-long tea culture to coffee, as well as a wuxia (martial arts fantasy) novella featuring Joan of Arc, in which the tropes and expectations of wuxia are mapped to Medieval Europe. These stories are extremely entertaining for the reader with the right cultural context and shed light on the genres and sources Ma plays with, but would be neigh-impenetrable for a reader in translation without extensive footnotes.

Then there's also Bao Shu, a celebrated new writer whose meteoric rise onto the scene during the last few years has been propelled by a series of inventive, funny, and moving short stories. Last year, Bao Shu published his debut novel, *The Ruins of Time,* which tells a tale of heroism and faith in a world trapped in a time loop, and which has just won the Xingyun (Nebula) Award for Chinese SF. Bao Shu's true "first" novel was a fanfiction sequel set in the world of Liu Cixin's *Three-Body* series, and the playful, pastiche-laden style he first demonstrated there remains a key part of his appeal—and gives his translators plenty of headaches.

This is but a cursory and shallow glance at the scene of contemporary Chinese science fiction. Time and space limitations prevent me from going into depth about the surreal imagery and metaphor-driven logic of Tang Fei, the dense, rich language-pictures painted by Cheng Jingbo, the fabulism and sociological speculation of Hao Jingfang, the gentle meditations on art and science by Wu Shuang (a.k.a. Anna Wu), or the rigorous historical imagination of Qian Lifang, whose *Will of Heaven,* a science fictional retelling of the founding of the Han Dynasty, was perhaps the most popular work of long-form science fiction in the pre-*Three Body* era.

I also haven't read enough to comment on other prominent writers such as Fei Dao, Jiang Bo, He Xi, and many others. And of course, I've said nothing here concerning the large number of *chuanyue* ("time travel") works, many of which also contain science fictional elements and deserve an essay on their own . . .

But this brief survey should give a hint of the broad range in the science fiction written in China. Faced with such variety, I think it is far more useful and interesting to study the authors as individuals and to treat their works on their own terms rather than trying to impose a pre-conceived set of expectations on them because they happen to be "Chinese science fiction."

Given the realities of China's politics and its uneasy relationship with the West, it is natural for Western readers encountering Chinese science fiction to see it through the lens of Western dreams and hopes and fairytales about Chinese politics. "Subversion" in the pro-West sense may become an interpretive crutch.

It is tempting, for example, to view Ma Boyong's "The City of Silence" as a simple attack on China's censorship apparatus, or to read Chen Qiufan's "The Year of the Rat" as just a criticism of China's education system and labor market, or even to reduce Xia Jia's "A Hundred Ghosts Parade Tonight" to a veiled metaphor for China's eminent domain policies in the service of state-driven development.

I would urge the reader to resist such temptation. Imagining that the political concerns of Chinese writers are the same as what the Western reader would like them to be is at best arrogant and at worst dangerous. Chinese writers are saying something about the globe, about all of humanity, not just China, and trying to understand their works through this perspective is, I think, the far more rewarding approach.

It is true that there is a long tradition in China of voicing dissent and criticism through the use of literary metaphor; however, this is but one of the purposes with which writers write and for which readers read. Like writers everywhere today, Chinese writers are concerned with humanism, with globalization, with technological advancement, with tradition and modernity, with disparities in wealth and privilege, with development and environmental preservation, with history, rights, freedom, and justice, with family and love, with the beauty of expressing sentiment through words, with language play, with the grandeur of science, with the thrill of discovery, with the ultimate meaning of life. We do the works a disservice when we neglect these things and focus on geopolitics alone.

Despite the diversity of approaches and subjects and styles, the authors and stories I have discussed (and especially those works that have made it into English translation) represent but a narrow slice of the contemporary Chinese science fiction landscape. As Xia Jia has said, "Contemporary Chinese science fiction writers form a community full of internal differences. These differences manifest themselves in age, region of origin, professional background, social class, ideology, cultural identity, aesthetics, and other areas."[4]

The stories that are translated tend to be written by authors who are graduates of China's most elite colleges and work in highly regarded professions. They tend to be award-winning stories rather than popular fiction published on the Web. And as I've already hinted at earlier, works that are translated tend to be more accessible than works requiring a deeper understanding of Chinese culture and history. These are unfortunate biases and omissions, and the reader should thus be cautious about any conclusions they may draw from the stories in translation being "representative."

China is dreaming, and its dreams contain multitudes.

Selected Bibliography of Contemporary Chinese SF Works in Translation

Individual Stories in Magazines or General Anthologies

- Chen Qiufan, "The Endless Farewell," *Pathlight*, Spring 2013, translated by Ken Liu.
- Chen Qiufan, "The Fish of Lijiang," *Clarkesworld*, August 2011, translated by Ken Liu.
- Chen Qiufan, "The Flower of Shazui," *Interzone*, October 2012, translated by Ken Liu.
- Chen Qiufan, "The Mao Ghost," *Lightspeed*, March 2014, translated by Ken Liu.
- Chen Qiufan, "Oil of Angels," *Upgraded*, edited by Neil Clarke, translated by Ken Liu.
- Chen Qiufan, "The Year of the Rat," *The Magazine of Fantasy and Science Fiction*, July/August 2013, translated by Ken Liu.
- Chen Qiufan, *The Waste Tide*. English translation by Ken Liu, forthcoming.
- Cheng Jingbo, "Grave of the Fireflies," *Clarkesworld*, January 2014, translated by Ken Liu.
- Hao Jingfang, "Invisible Planets," *Lightspeed*, December 2013, translated by Ken Liu.
- Hao Jingfang, "Folding Beijing," *Uncanny*, 2015, translated by Ken Liu.
- Liu Cixin, *The Three-Body Problem*, Tor Books, 2014, translated by Ken Liu.
- Liu Cixin, "Taking Care of God," *Pathlight*, April 2012.

- Ma Boyong, "The City of Silence," *World SF Blog,* November 2011, translated by Ken Liu.
- Ma Boyong, "Mark Twain Robots," *TRSF* (September 2011), a special publication of MIT's *Technology Review,* translated by Ken Liu.
- Qian Lifang, *Will of Heaven,* translated by "WoH Translator."
- Tang Fei, "Call Girl," *Apex,* June 2013, translated by Ken Liu.
- Tang Fei, "Pepe," *Clarkesworld,* June 2014, translated by John Chu.
- Xia Jia, "A Hundred Ghosts Parade Tonight," *Clarkesworld,* February 2012, translated by Ken Liu.
- Xia Jia, "Spring Festival: Happiness, Anger, Love, Sorrow, Joy," *Clarkesworld,* September 2012, translated by Ken Liu.
- Xia Jia, "Tongtong's Summer," *Upgraded,* ed. Neil Clarke, 2014, translated by Ken Liu.
- Zhao Haihong, "Exuviation," *Lady Churchill's Rosebud Wristlet,* 2010 (reprinted by *Lightspeed,* January 2014.

Journals or Anthologies Specializing in Works in Translation

The Apex Book of World SF, edited by Lavie Tidhar, 2009. Includes
- Han Song, "The Wheel of Samsara"
- Yang Ping, "Wizard World"

The Apex Book of World SF, Volume 2, edited by Lavie Tidhar, 2012. Includes
- Chen Qiufan, "The Tomb"
- Yang Ping, "Wizard World"

RENDITIONS A Chinese-English Translation Magazine Nos. 77 & 78—Spring and Autumn 2012, edited by Mingwei Song. This double issue contains both works from the early twentieth century and the early twenty-first century. The more relevant contemporary works include:
- Liu Cixin, "The Poetry Cloud," translated by Chi-yin Ip and Cheuk Wong
- Liu Cixin, "The Village Schoolteacher," translated by Christopher Elford and Jiang Chenxin
- Han Song, "The Passengers and the Creator," translated by Nathaniel Isaacson
- Wang Jinkang, "The Reincarnated Giant," translated by Carlos Rojas
- La La, "The Radio Waves That Never Die," translated by Petula Parris-Huang

- Zhao Haihong, "1923—a Fantasy," translated by Nicky Harman and Pang Zhaoxia
- Chi Hui, "The Rainforest," translated by Jie Li
- Fei Dao, "The Demon's Head," translated by David Hull
- Xia Jia, "The Demon-Enslaving Flask," translated by Linda Rui Feng

FOOTNOTES:

1 Figures obtained from Gardner Dozois' 2013 summation in his *Year's Best Science Fiction, Thirty-First Annual Collection.*

2 A selected bibliography is given at the end of this essay so that readers may find some of these works.

3 For more on the history of Chinese science fiction, see Xia Jia's essay, "What Makes Chinese Science Fiction Chinese?" July 22, 2014, *Tor.com.*

4 Xia Jia, "What Makes Chinese Science Fiction Chinese?" July 22, 2014, *Tor. com.*

ABOUT THE AUTHOR

Ken Liu is an author and translator of speculative fiction, as well as a lawyer and programmer. A winner of the Nebula, Hugo, and World Fantasy Awards, he has been published in *The Magazine of Fantasy & Science Fiction, Asimov's, Analog, Clarkesworld, Lightspeed,* and *Strange Horizons,* among other places. He lives with his family near Boston, Massachusetts.

Ken's debut novel, *The Grace of Kings,* the first in a silkpunk epic fantasy series, will be published by Saga Press, Simon & Schuster's new genre fiction imprint, in April 2015. Saga will also publish a collection of his short stories.

In Civilized Society: A Conversation with Kameron Hurley

ALVARO ZINOS-AMARO

I first learned of Kameron Hurley's work when Jeff VanderMeer wrote about *God's War* as one of his top books from 2011 in a piece for *Locus*. He referred to the novel's "fascinating insect-based tech" and "unique cultural underpinnings," which pretty much sold me right there. He also noted that Hurley's prose was "muscular," which further intrigued me. For readers who don't know the series, I'll add that Nyx, the protagonist, is a character with whom it's impossible *not* to develop a relationship—though I won't say of what type.

As someone who enjoys non-fiction related to science fiction, I was (doubly?) impressed when, at the most recent WorldCon, Kameron was awarded with two Hugos for her non-fiction: one for Best Fan Writer and one for Best Related Work, for her essay " 'We Have Always Fought': Challenging the 'Women, Cattle and Slaves' Narrative." You can find this piece, and much else besides, in her non-fiction collection, *We Have Always Fought: Essays on Writing, Craft and Fandom* (2014).

These days whenever I download the latest copy of *Locus,* one of the first things I do is click through to see if there's a new commentary piece by Kameron—they are invariably impassioned and thought-provoking.

Kameron Hurley is the two-time Hugo awarding winning author of *The Mirror Empire* and the science fantasy noir *God's War* Trilogy. The trilogy earned her a Kitschy Award for best Debut Novel, Sydney J. Bounds Award for Best Newcomer, and a Nebula and Locus Award nomination. She has lived in Washington, Alaska, Ohio, Chicago, and Durban, South Africa. Her short fiction has appeared in magazines such as *Lightspeed, EscapePod* and *Strange Horizons,* as well as the anthologies *Year's Best SF, The Mammoth Book of SF by Women,* and*The Lowest Heaven.* Her work has been translated into Romanian, Swedish, Chinese, Spanish and Russian. She also writes a regular column for *Locus Magazine* and blogs at kameronhurley.com.

You've described science fiction as being better at inspiring rather than predicting the future. Are there any specific SF/F works that helped inspire you when you were young? If so, what were they, and how did that inspiration manifest?

My first career aspiration was to be an astronaut. Like a lot of kids growing up in the 80's I found myself in a culture still stuffed full of interest in the stars, fueled by the legacy of the Cold War. We still broadcast shuttle launches. People still cared. Star Trek films and old episodes played endlessly in my household, and *Star Trek: The Next Generation* was gaining steam. I sat up watching apocalypse and dystopian movies, too, *Mad Max* and *Cyborg* and *Neon City* and *Robocop,* which reminded me I'd need a little more grit in the face of a less hopeful future.

I came to written science fiction rather late, in my late teens and early twenties. And then I devoured old classics from Bester to Russ to Butler to LeGuin to Delany. Many of the technologies we see today were inspired by those earlier works; from the internet to our pocket computer/communication devices. Alas, I often feel some of our politicians took the grim social futures of those dystopian apocalypses as a guidebook as opposed to a warning, but—you win some, you lose some.

Can you say a few words about how the history of resistance move-

ments, which you've studied academically, may have influenced your fiction and non-fiction?

I spent my undergraduate and graduate years immersed in the history of women's roles in resistance movements, particular in Southern Africa. Digging into that uncovered a whole other history I hadn't seen much of until then. That being the history where women did things instead of just having things done to them. It got me to start interrogating how we talk about women and people of color in our own history—are they the people being "helped" or "uplifted" (ha) by European men, or are they active participants in their own stories, fighting to perpetuate or simply maintain their cultural identity? It was my first real foray into a worldview outside the one I was spoon-fed by the wider American culture, and it forced me to challenge everything that came before and after it.

Naturally, that need to question assumptions and stories created by those with their own political agendas bled over into my fiction. I spend a lot of time asking if I'm just perpetuating lazy attitudes because I've swallowed them whole cloth or if I'm really interrogating and imagining something different. I'm a science fiction and fantasy writer. If I can't unshackle myself from bad cultural programming, what hope is there?

You've observed that all writing is political. How do you balance an awareness of your own writing as political with your desire to tell an engaging, entertaining story?

The assumption here is that one can't tell an engaging and entertaining story while being political. But I'd argue all of Bradbury's work is political—those 1950's housewife Martian women making breakfast while the husband reads the paper? That simple scene dumps a whole bunch of political assumptions on us immediately. And Orwell posits that a totalitarian communist state would be just horrible, a dystopia, which we accept without really questioning it. It was many years before I thought, well, why does it have to be horrible? Surely we can imagine a totalitarian communist state that some people actually really like? Goodness knows I often feel like we're living in a capitalist dystopia. One person's dystopia is another's utopia, after all. And let's not even get started with Ayn Rand.

But I understand what people are getting at when they ask me this question, because there's certainly some old-school feminist science fiction that is just sort of people wandering around looking at plants, or thinking about how much better the world is now that they aren't oppressed. But there are loads of really boring male power fantasy books where guys just wander around in space wishing they could actually feel emotions anymore while they shoot things, and we consider those deep and important books worth giving awards to, so clearly there's a bit of a double standard there.

What I wanted to do was bring all the things I loved about feminist science fiction—new ways of organizing societies, challenging cultural mores, inventive marriages, complex families—and blend that with what I loved from a lot of other science fiction and epic fantasy; explosions, invaders, political maneuvering, angst, impossible odds, crazy magic, wild tech.

I'd like to say this isn't a difficult thing to do, but having done it over four books now, I have to admit it's really draining. You're not only building a whole physical world with a new tech and/or magic system, but you're creating wholly new societies, not just "Oh, these are the pseudo-medieval Europeans" or "Oh, these are the pseudo-medieval Japanese folks" but actually creating wholly new societies mashed up from bits and pieces of both historical societies and stuff you just make up yourself. It takes a tremendous amount of effort to reimagine and re-interrogate the world from the ground up, let me tell you.

But in the end, it's very satisfying.

You just used the word "reimagine," and it reminds me of an image I enjoyed in a recent non-fiction piece you published in Fantasy magazine: "I've reimagined cheese not as some pale lumps covered in pea sprouts but a full-on Spanish cheese sampler." When you're engaged in the creative process, do you do this primarily in the early planning stages of a story, or as you go, layer by layer? Has that process changed since you started?

I go layer by layer. The first pass through, my worlds read as pretty standard ones, I think. I came up with the first line to *God's War* before I knew anything else about the world or the person except that Nyx was a bounty hunter and I wanted something set in the desert. So I had, "Nyx sold her womb somewhere between Punjai and Faleen, on the edge of the desert," and then just started building the world from there. I didn't create a map until I was a good hundred pages into the novel, when it seemed like something that might stick. It took four years to write a draft, but the real magic happened in the re-writing. I'd go back through my research notes and add in details about how people lived and dressed; I added in air raids and acid guns.

I'm writing the sequel to *The Mirror Empire, Empire Ascendant* right now, and it's mostly dialogue and fight scenes at this point. There are some key plants—a giant living mountain that eats people, and a scene where a plant devours someone from the inside out—but for the most part, the real sticky details regarding social interactions and flora and fauna will come in during the final few passes.

So that layer-by-layer process is something that hasn't really changed for me the last few years. If I tried to write really detailed worldbuilding and weird cultures on the first pass, I don't think I'd ever finish a draft. But once you have a draft in place, it's a lot easier to layer all the rest of that over the story. I also think that's one reason I've been able to avoid having the world totally overtake the story, which is a common problem people see in fantasy especially—the story and characters come first, and then the world gets layered on over the top. The worldbuilding is always the scene-setting for the story, the story doesn't just exist to showcase the world.

Your passion comes through in everything you write. How have you managed to keep your passion alive and prevent burnout over the years, through the practical vicissitudes of a writing career?

I've only been writing a book a year since 2011, so let's not rule out burnout yet! Avoiding burnout has been tremendously difficult. Not because of the actual writing, but the business side of writing—contracts, promotion, marketing, business wrangling, publishing relationships. Keeping up with all of that on top of the book a year, and all of that on top of a day job, has been a terrifying balancing act, and I don't always manage it.

I spend a lot of time scheduling set amounts of time for particular activities. Like, this two months is for promotion, and this six months is for writing. When I'm in promo mode I do very little writing, and when I'm in writing mode, I do very little promo. To be honest, I'm not sure how much longer I'll be able to do a book a year. I'm contracted through 2018 to write a book a year, so, maybe until 2018. Ha!

You've talked about having to find ways to hack your own process to work faster, since you have a day job etc. What are some successful hacks you've discovered that you can share with us?

I read Rachel Aaron's "2k to 10k" where she talks about how she hacked her writing process so she can now write up to 10,000 words a day. She has a lot of helpful advice about finding the right time of day, and logging your word count, but the best advice I found was to write a few sentences about the scene you're sitting down to write before you write it. I'm a very organic writer, and my outlines are pretty loose. Unfortunately, that means I can often spend my entire writing time writing page after page of two characters talking about tax law over tea. And that's just not . . . terribly interesting. It also isn't going to get the novel done faster.

Setting down a few sentences before I write each scene was a nice compromise for me between serious outlining and just letting things happen as they happened. I didn't have to write down what would happen in every chapter beforehand, or stick rigidly to a massive outline, but I did need to ensure that when I sat down to write, all of the major events in those two or three sentences happened within that scene. It made it a lot easier to move the plot forward with every scene, instead of spending page after page figuring out what I wanted to say and then cutting out all the rest later.

How does it feel to have won two Hugo awards recently for your non-fiction?

Surreal, still. They haven't arrived yet, so I don't think it's really sunk in yet, believe it or not. The Hugo was the one award I figured I'd never win. It's an award made by popular vote, and folks in the industry had told me for a long time that I was a niche writer. But the community as a whole has been very supportive of the work I do, both the fiction and nonfiction, and that's been very gratifying. It makes the tough days worth it.

Your three Bel Dame Apocrypha novels—God's War (2011), Infidel (2011), and Rapture (2012)—are in the New Weird tradition. Your latest novel, The Mirror Empire (2014), the first in your new World-breaker Saga, seems to be closer to epic fantasy. Is that right? What led you from one sensibility to the other?

I wrote many drafts of what would become *The Mirror Empire* before I wrote *God's War*. I'd tried to sell *The Mirror Empire* first, but had very little interest. It was 200,000 words back then, very wordy, with very little plot. The characters were the same, but the magic system felt more like something out of *The Wheel of Time* and the societies were much more clearly pseudo-medieval. There was simply nothing about the book that stood out in the marketplace. It read a lot like a travelogue.

With *God's War* I decided to blow open the doors on what I thought I should write and just throw everything in there, since trying to play by the bland, boring rules wasn't getting my work published anyway. *God's War* has magicians and aliens and shapeshifters and spaceships. So though it's on the SF side, it's certainly not a world anyone would say was rooted in scientific fact.

When I revisited *The Mirror Empire* after I finished the Bel Dame books, I decided to take the same approach of just throwing in everything I loved instead of holding back and trying to write something everyone else was writing. So there are parallel worlds and swords and satellites and blood mages. I don't much believe that there's a difference between science fiction and fantasy, and that shows up in what I write. When I choose a marketing bucket for a particular book, I just choose the genre it looks the most like instead of trying to explain how it's a mash-up. People have a real aversion to genre mash-ups, at least if you market them that way.

The funny thing is that for years and years I tried to write very safe sorts of books and stories because those were the books I'd see on the shelves. When I started reading weirder books and let myself just write what I wanted to write instead of feeling like I should write what other people wanted me to write, well, that's when I finally started selling my work reliably.

I've heard you say that when someone gets caught up in whether your work is science fiction or fantasy, you tell them, "It's ThunderCats!" If you could be a ThunderCats character, who would you pick, and why?

I admit I've always been partial to Lion-O, who reminds me a lot of the character of Ahkio in *The Mirror Empire*—this sort of reluctant, nice-guy leader hero who means well, but maybe could use a little more wisdom, and looks to solve problems through happy resolutions instead of violence, mostly.

I wouldn't say he's at all like me in the least, but being a nice person who can help resolve people's problems without wanting to whack them in the head is something to aspire to in civilized society.

Or so I hear.

ABOUT THE AUTHOR

Alvaro Zinos-Amaro is the co-author, with Robert Silverberg, of *When the Blue Shift Comes*, which received a starred review from *Library Journal*. Alvaro's short fiction and poetry have appeared or are forthcoming in *Analog, Nature, Galaxy's Edge, Apex* and other venues, and Alvaro was nominated for the 2013 Rhysling Award. Alvaro's reviews, critical essays and interviews have appeared in *The Los Angeles Review of Books, Strange Horizons, SF Signal, The New York Review of Science Fiction, Foundation,* and other markets. Alvaro currently edits the blog for *Locus*.

Another Word: Endings

DANIEL ABRAHAM

Endings are hard.

There are a lot of reasons for that. First off, figuring out just technically how to stick an ending is nearly the last thing that a writer has to figure out. All the other stuff—writing a good sentence, writing a good scene, the tricky bit with adverbs, avoiding infodumps, celebrating infodumps, being confused about infodumps, all of it—is complicated enough to fill a lifetime. And since even rock-solid structure won't save you if the prose bounces people off in the first couple pages, it's not a priority. Learn how to write a good hook, and you at least get the **chance** to whiff the ending. With a crap hook, no one gets to the middle, much less the end.

More than that, errors that are hard to see at the beginning often show up at the ending. Brilliant short story writer Jim van Pelt once told me that whenever someone said there was a problem with the end of his story, it meant there was a problem with the setup of his story.

If some sense of the character didn't quite land in the third scene, the place you'll know it is at the end. If the pacing in the middle wasn't right, you'll know it at the end. Not because the end itself is particularly good or bad in its own right, but because once the last paragraph is read and the dream of the story ends, that's the time when as a reader, you can reflect on the whole experience of the story. Did it work, did it not? Are you moved, are you satisfied, are you bored? In that moment of evaluation, all the flaws and failings appear, even if you don't know exactly what they were.

But that's not the only reason endings are hard.

Even the most successful ending to a story carries a sense of loss. As a reader, we've been deep in this other place with characters and moments that enthralled us and with every new moment, every revelation, every turned page, the distance to the back cover grows thinner. Until you run out of words, and the story's done, can you then evaluate what happened. The worst case scenario is relief. At least that damned book's done and you can go on to something that'll clear it out of your head. But if it worked, there's a satisfaction and regret. We'll miss those characters. Those places. Even if we feel satisfied and full, something we enjoyed is gone now. Maybe we start the reread right then to get it back, or download the second volume of the series onto our e-book reader right there in bed. Something to prolong the experience, to make the ending not an ending, because endings are hard.

When I was about ten, I read the Narnia books. They hit at pretty much exactly the right time for me, because I fell through them one after another right up until *The Last Battle.* Which I've never read. I wasn't ready for the story to be over, and so I stopped. As long as I didn't read that one last book, the story would never end.

And, over the last few decades, the kid who read those books has turned into just me, so even if I do sit down with it now, it won't be the same thing it would have been then. That story was saved from ending because I wasn't ready to let the sense of possibility go. But that's only part of why endings are hard.

Endings are hard because people die. I've been lucky so far, but that's just timing and we all know it. Grandma Garner, whose house I stayed every Friday night from when I was five until I was maybe fourteen, is dead. Grandpa Garner died while I was at the house with him. Jay Lake is gone, and he was a friend. Eugie Foster is gone. Graham Joyce. My parents are still alive. My wife is still alive. My daughter is. They're all going to go, myself as well. And we don't even know the order.

Margaret Atwood says it in her short story or maybe essay "Happy Endings." "The only authentic ending is the one provided here: John and Mary die, John and Mary die, John and Mary die." It's something we all know and we all struggle with and we all dread. The melancholy of ending a brilliant story isn't that different from the melancholy of remembering that kid who was scarfing down C. S Lewis until his nerve failed him. He's gone now. The room he lived in isn't the same space it was. The loves and fears he had don't apply. The inevitability of the past, of all these things moving into the past, makes an ending—an authentic, powerful, successful ending also a presentiment of death. Every closed book is also a memento mori. But that's not the only reason endings are hard. The biggest reason—the most important reason I think, that endings are hard is that we're trained off them.

I am profoundly grateful to live in a secular society. I just want to get that out up front. I love living someplace where people can worship God differently, have different views of the essential nature of the universe, debate science and poetry and art, and where all of that can be part of a larger, richer secular culture that has the potential to celebrate the whole range of humanity. Way better than theocracy every time. Not saying it makes everything perfect. Not saying it's without blemishes.

For instance, the news.

News is the privileged narrative of a secular society. It defines what information is important — what stories matter. Turning away from the news in a modern secular culture is as weird and isolating and rebellious as not going to church would have been in more religious times. It is where we turn to know what matters: that is its role and its justification. And here's the thing. It doesn't do endings.

Malaysian Airlines Flight 370 went missing in March of 2014, and for months was the main story at CNN. People speculated that it had been taken by terrorists as part of some larger scheme, or that it had been downed as a suicide by one of the pilots, or failed because of a bizarre confluence of equipment failure and human error. Or abducted by aliens. Whatever the details of the particular analysis, simply by being in the headlines, the subtext we all got was the same: this is important. And then ... no resolution came. Like reading a novel with an amazing first chapter that sagged into nothing in the middle, the story didn't resolve. It was interrupted by other things which were **by their presence** clearly more important. More recently ISIS and Ebola followed the same pattern. The issues were headline news until they were interrupted by snow storms and the collapse of Bill Cosby and whatever great hook of a story comes next. Our central cultural narrative is desperately empty of resolutions. Instead, it is one of interruption. Of issues brought up, obsessed over, and then put aside for more pressing matters, forever, eternally.

Endlessly.

That is the world we practice. A world in which resolution is less important than a new hook, in which endings are so optional that when we skip over them—What happened with ISIS? What happened to the guys behind the housing crisis? Where did the missing plane go?—they aren't even missed. We look back at the unresolved threads of that were so critical to us six months or a year ago with a kind of nostalgia, like "Oh, I remember that. Whatever became of it?" And slowly, over years and decades, we're trained that endings are optional. That we don't need them. That they're hard.

If there is something that fiction offers, it's this: stories end. In fiction, unlike anyplace else, the narrative takes its form, the characters play their parts, and the author brings it all together to the point she intended from the beginning, and by ending, they make a kind of meaning that we don't get anywhere else. We can experience (even if it's only in miniature) what it would be like for things— stories, lives—to have meaning.

> "The good ended happily, the bad unhappily.
> That's what fiction means."
> —Oscar Wilde

ABOUT THE AUTHOR

Daniel Abraham is a writer of genre fiction with a dozen books in print and over thirty published short stories. His work has been nominated for the Nebula, World Fantasy, and Hugo Awards and has been awarded the International Horror Guild Award. He also writes as MLN Hanover and (with Ty Franck) as James S. A. Corey. He lives in the American Southwest.

Editor's Desk:
Giant Heads

NEIL CLARKE

So why are Sean and I holding those scary-looking silver heads? Last month, Sean, Kate and I won a World Fantasy Award for our work on *Clarkesworld*! (Sadly, Kate was unable to attend the ceremony.)

I'd like to thank our readers for their help in making it possible for us to publish this magazine. Without your subscriptions, donations, or other kinds of support, this wouldn't be possible.

From all of us here at *Clarkesworld*, we hope you have a wonderful month, happy holidays (should you celebrate), and a fantastic end to your year. See you next month for our big issue #100 celebration!

ABOUT THE AUTHOR

Neil Clarke is the editor of *Clarkesworld Magazine,* owner of Wyrm Publishing and a three-time Hugo Award Nominee for Best Editor (short form). He currently lives in NJ with his wife and two children.

About the Artist
LAKE HURWITZ

Lake Hurwitz a professional illustrator and concept artist currently located in Seattle. His professional skill set draws from a passion for the expansive worlds within, coupled with love for video games and classical art. In the past he studied first at Ringling College of Art and Design, and then at The Safehouse Atelier with Carl Dobsky and the concept art studio Massive Black. They taught the understanding of form and light, as well as a healthy respect for a production pipeline. All these experiences have taught Lake the portrayal of form to a height of realism, and also a good understanding of graphic shape and thoughtful design. He is a fan of horror, fantasy, and science fiction alike.

WEBSITE

demonui.com